MW01536621

A RIVETING INVESTIGATIVE THRILLER

NITI KEWALRAMANI

Srishti
PUBLISHERS & DISTRIBUTORS

Srishti Publishers & Distributors
A unit of AJR Publishing LLP
212A, Peacock Lane
Shahpur Jat, New Delhi – 110 049

editorial@srishtipublishers.com

First published by
Srishti Publishers & Distributors in 2023

Copyright © Niti Kewalramani, 2023

10 9 8 7 6 5 4 3 2 1

This is a work of fiction. The characters, places, organisations and events described in this book are either a work of the author's imagination or have been used fictitiously. Any resemblance to people, living or dead, places, events, communities or organisations is purely coincidental.

The author asserts the moral right to be identified as the author of this work.

All rights reserved. No part of this publication may be reproduced, stored in a retrieval system, or transmitted, in any form or by any means, electronic, mechanical, photocopying, recording or otherwise, without the prior written permission of the Publishers.

Printed and bound in India

For my parents

Acknowledgements

This book took way too long to see the light of day, and it would have taken longer had it not been for my incredible publishing team:

@ Suhail Mathur (The Book Bakers Literary Agency): Thank you for helping me navigate this unchartered territory. I am amazed at your quick response time to my queries. There have been many.

@ Stuti Gupta and Arup Bose from Srishti Publishers: I am grateful for your belief, encouragement, and sparkle. As a debutant novelist, I have asked more than my share of 'dumb questions,' but you guys have been ever-patient, kind, and supportive. I appreciate all you have done for me - a special shout-out to the design team for a fantastic cover.

To my readers, I thank you for entering my world and entrusting me with your attention. Your support means a lot to me.

I am beyond grateful to...

Althea Kaushal, who, in the early days of the idea, very diligently read everything I sent her and then politely suggested I discard at least half of it. Your unabashed honesty is immensely cherished.

ACP Ram Deshmukh, Virar Division, Mira Bhyander Vasai Virar Commissionerate, Mumbai Police, who gave me his valuable time and fact-checked some details.

Anjum Rajabali @ Whistling Woods for his unparalleled knowledge and limitless enthusiasm for the art of storytelling.

Sir, you are a master of the craft. Your teachings have endeared you into many hearts.

Anish Chandy, for his clever strike-outs on the earlier drafts.

My students, I am forever learning something new from them.

Mira, Sumeet, Donna, Manjula, and Mock for being integral to my journey.

My cherished friends for always encouraging me and supporting my creative pursuits. A special thank you to Saanika Gandhi for the intense title buzz sessions and many other deliberations.

And finally, I am forever indebted to Girish, Aman, and Abhir for being the first readers and my go-to team for everything. I am grateful for your incisive edits, biting commentary, cheeky roasts, and cheerful toasts. I got there because of you and chocolate.

Chapter 1
Surya

Zanara
Mumbai, 17th June 2016

The landline's shrill ring echoed through the corridors for a long time before it seeped into her consciousness. Sharda stirred on her 400-thread count silk bedsheet and reached for her mobile. It was seven a.m. Her mind, though groggy, did the math. It had only been seven hours since she had taken the Xanax. Another sixty minutes and she would have extracted the full value from these addictive benzodiazepines. Except now, she could almost hear her husband berating her: *500 dollars for a box of pills? They'd better be fucking worth it.* He was clearly doing justice to his pill as he snored beside her.

The screaming phone caught her attention, jolting her back to her senses.

"Hello," she said, yawning.

"Hello Sharda ji, this is Prakash Yadav, Commissioner of Police. May I speak with MJ *sahib* or Ashok sir? I'm unable to reach either of them."

"Namaste, Prakash ji. *Babuji* must be busy with his yoga and —" she hesitated, as she was not comfortable uttering her husband's name for fear of shortening his longevity, "My husband has been resting since the *tula daan.* Did something happen?" she asked.

There was a pause.

"Sharda ji, it is better that I speak with MJ sahib first."

A sliver of irritation crept into her voice. "What is it that you cannot tell *me*, Prakash ji?"

He hesitated.

"I am very sorry, but your son Surya Jain is... dead."

Chapter 2
MJ

Zanara
Mumbai, 16th June 2016

Growling, the Rolls Royce moved slowly, bullying the cars and the cyclewalas to give way. It pulled up in the driveway of Zanara, the Jains' abode in Mumbai. Zanara was built on Altamount Road, Mumbai's most expensive pin code. Unlike other residences, it was the only one built entirely on one level. The walls and hedges around this coy beauty stood as a fortress shielding it from the roving eyes of the public.

The doors of the Rolls Royce swung open to reveal Motilal Jain, aka MJ, a man preserved in sartorial splendour. As he stepped out in his white-coloured, double-vested suit, his 1960s fedora was caught off guard by an unannounced breeze that unsettled his sparse strands of usually well-behaved hair. Immediately regaining his composure, MJ pasted his hair down with a firm hand, as if admonishing it for this act of betrayal.

Today was an important day for MJ. His son, Ashok was celebrating his fiftieth birthday. As a new parent, MJ had been ecstatic when he had first held baby Ashok in his arms. This 'white as milk' cherub, who weighed an astonishing 4.1 kilos and was 59 centimetres long, was undoubtedly a divine sanction, as such chroma and proportions were unheard of in the Jain community. Bhanu Priya had arrived three years later, possessing ordinary body measurements. He had sensed that

3

her life was destined to be like her dimensions. But as the years passed, MJ realised that Ashok was just as ordinary.

Unlike his children, MJ had been special. Young Motilal had built his kingdom one sand grain at a time. Established on the barren hinterlands of Dubai, Saachi Group International (SGI) was a success story with a turnover of 700 million USD, employing more than 1000 employees worldwide. MJ had returned to India in 1999 with a reverence beyond his wildest imagination. Headquartered in Mumbai, SGI had grown from strength to strength, but lately, its future was shrouded in doubt. The company had an aging king at the helm. MJ knew he had to announce a new leader soon.

Walking towards the patio, he paused for a second to behold the beauty of Zanara. Covered entirely in strings of marigolds, Zanara's main entrance was like a bride's veil, teasing the onlooker, but yielding nothing. MJ was pleased that he had given Sharda, his *bahu*, a free hand in planning the entire event. Sharda had been thrilled at the opportunity and had even made some outlandish suggestions. But it had all fallen into place.

As he drifted inside his bright living room resplendent of a Rajasthani haveli, he encountered a magnificent gold-plated weighing scale lounging carefree under the room's central chandelier. A little to its left was a two-seater sofa and to its right, a *sandook* made of cast iron. This custom-made chest was brimming with real jewellery, gold coins, and money.

Suddenly, MJ heard frenzied chanting. He noticed a dwarfish, pot-bellied *pujari* going about his business with a *havan kundli*. MJ's entry had awakened the lazing events team as well, who rushed to gather their *aarti thalis, tikkas,* and other colourful weaponry to welcome him. He checked his watch; there was still an hour before the guests would arrive. Waving his arms in protest against an advancing garland, MJ headed straight to his room.

Chapter 3
Chana

Zanara
Mumbai, 16th June 2016

Chana was dressed in an Indian outfit that usually awaited its time to be summoned around Diwali. Clasping a pearl necklace over her georgette kurta, she conceded that she would probably need to invest in another outfit this year. A saree, perhaps? She would ask one of the ladies from her Pilates class to help her sort it out. Most of the ladies belonged to the upper echelons of society, but that didn't stop them from putting an outfit together piecemeal: fabric, lace, buttons, lining, and finally, haggling with the tailor to reduce the price.

Chana had experimented with many variations of this outfit before; she was pairing it with beige slacks today. Since it was going to be a prayer ceremony, she knew she would need to carry something to cover her head. Being promoted as PA to MJ, the most important man in the SGI universe, she had dived headlong into the Jains' belief systems. Old Vedic views had a prominent seat, even in SGI's ultra-modern offices. All three men active in the business – MJ, his son Ashok, and his grandson Surya – were vegetarians and teetotallers, at least in public. MJ had even hired a Chief Belief Officer, a dhoti and printed shirt adorning old fart, who spat Sanskrit words unifying personal beliefs with the company's mission.

Unimpressive as he was, the CBO did have a knack of linking random concepts such as dharma to dividends and asuras to absenteeism. SGI placed vegetarianism at the centre of its advertising strategy, and MJ was clearly the poster boy. The gods must have been pleased with MJ, as SGI became one of India's fastest-growing FMCG companies.

Growing up, Chana, half Indian and half Italian, had not practiced any religion. But in her current job, her employment contract even stipulated the days she had to practice vegetarianism. Fasting during navratri was compulsory, and an additional 180 days fell under the 'highly recommended' category. But she didn't mind it. Her love affair with Indian gods had begun when she had accompanied the carb-faced SGI bahu, Sharda, to the clan's Kul Devi temple, a five-hour drive from Mumbai. She spotted liquor stores selling imported and country varieties dotted along the temple's periphery. Sharda handed two Chivas Regal bottles wrapped in newspapers to the temple priest, who offered the drink to the goddess in a saucer. *You can never be sure of the quality, that's why we always carry our own*, Sharda had said to her.

Before leaving her one-bedroom apartment, Chana picked up a green shawl and gently placed it on her shoulder. Immediately, there was a chaos of colours, an unforeseen tiff between the clashing tones that settled as soon as she unpinned her brown hair that cascaded down her shoulders and neutralised all the parties. Finally, there was harmony.

Inside her Uber, she pulled out the invitation card. A famous contemporary artist had been commissioned to create it for the event. Chana stared at it again to make sense of the heady cocktail of *kumkum*, big eyes, and tar stains that were smeared across the card. Her eyes rested on:

16 June 2016
Tula Daan
10:30 a.m. - 2 p.m.
Puja followed by Lunch

It was only ten a.m.; there was still plenty of time to reach Zanara and welcome the guests. She wondered about the tula daan. *Any* event, other than their annual Diwali celebrations, was an anomaly for the public-shy Jains. Unlike India's wealthiest who lived down the lane on Altamount Road, the Jains did not throw parties. Nor did they approve of filmi bahus or edible gold leaves in their Louis XIII cognac, or even cognac, for that matter. Even for their Diwali function, the meal was always homecooked, and served to a humble list of India's twenty-five wealthiest and most influential couples. Those jet-setting Mumbaikars worth their weight in bitcoin, who managed to secure an invite, happily picked the onion-and-garlic-free *dal baati churma* and *rooh afza* over parties that bragged multi-cuisine live stations and mobile bars manned by blonde apsara-like hostesses.

'Money shouts, wealth whispers' had been MJ's mantra. But for today's guest list, it was as if Sharda had swept a broom across Mumbai, and had collected in her dust-pan, reality show-slappers to politicians and everyone else in between. Chana was curious to discover why MJ had suddenly wanted his soft-spoken wealth to scream.

At 10:20 a.m., Chana's Uber sped through the Zanara gates. Once inside the mansion, Chana almost gasped at the setup. It was the first time she had seen such an outrageous show of riches by the Jains.

"Thank god, you are here. Now tell me, did you really hand-deliver all the invites?" Sharda asked, a hint of suspicion showing.

"Of course," Chana replied, dazzling Sharda with her kilowatt smile. "Why? Did something happen?"

"No one has called to get an inside scoop. Nobody from media is queuing up either."

"Oh, *that!*" Chana replied. "MJ had instructed that the media be allowed only if they are invitees. That strategy always works. Don't worry, your event will be a big hit." She smiled reassuringly.

Soon the first guests arrived. It was the US Counsel General and his wife. As this was the Counsel General's first posting to India, he was not accustomed to Indian Standard Time. His wife, Jane was wearing a hot-pink coloured salwar kameez by a popular designer. Chana gave her a 5/10.

"Thank you so much for coming," Sharda said, clasping both her hands in hers.

"Oh, we wouldn't miss it for anything. Can you please explain what a tula daan is?" Jane asked.

"Well, tula means scale, and daan means charity. It is an old Hindu practice of giving donations equivalent to one's weight. This tula daan puja is being performed for my husband, who will sit on one side of the weighing scale, and on the other side, we will keep adding wealth until the scale's balance is restored. Usually, people offer eatables like rice, wheat, pulses, sugar, and sometimes even metals like bronze and copper. But we decided to donate gold, jewels, and money," she said, pointing to the trunk. "We will be donating roughly seventy kilos of wealth to the poor."

"He only weighs seventy kilos? With our obesity rates, it's good that Americans don't follow this tradition," Jane observed.

"But what is the purpose of this ritual?" the Counsel General enquired.

"This puja will ward off the evil eye and any obstacles that may come in his way towards his new career," Sharda replied.

Chana wondered about Ashok's current career. Even at the age of fifty, Ashok appeared to be a puppet entirely in his father's control.

"Oh! A new career? Is he quitting the family business?" Jane asked innocently.

"Why will he leave the family business?" Sharda laughed nervously. "He is just going to actively involve himself with *samajseva*. He wants to serve his people, his community."

Chana almost choked on her rose sherbet.

"Excuse me," Sharda said, as she noticed MJ emerge from his bedroom in a crisp white dhoti and kurta. Bhanu Priya, his daughter was right beside him.

"I need to attend to my father-in-law," she said, subconsciously pulling the ends of her saree over her head.

"Oh, *Didi*, at least today, you should have decked up a little bit," Sharda complained to Bhanu.

"*Bhabhi*, this *is* a new dress, and it is expensive too!" Bhanu laughed.

Chana checked her out. Though it was a cotton dress, it was not that dull, she concluded. But Bhanu had a face that could make anything look boring.

Chana caught Ashok dawdling about in the living room.

"Chana, can you find out why it is so hot; check the ACs, please?" Sharda instructed, wiping off the pool of sweat forming on her brow.

"You should be checking that on your own, without being told," Ashok growled at Chana.

"I will look into it immediately," Chana said, and rushed off. Chana despised Ashok. He was like a satellite bully, always hanging around for an opportune moment to berate someone.

At 11 am, the room was brimming with people when Surya made his entry. Looking dapper in an ivory-white printed silk kurta, he strode across the living room and headed straight towards his grandfather to touch his feet. The Nehru jacket and red rose added to the setting. His twenty-five years had kissed him in all the right places. As if it was not enough for one man to be so good-looking, god had also teased his right cheek with a dimple.

MJ cleared his throat, and quickly the hubbub died down to a whisper.

"Good morning, my respectful friends. Thank you for taking the time to come to this puja. If my wife were alive today, she would have been proud as it is an exceptional day for us – our Ashok, our firstborn, turns fifty. He has always wanted to serve the country and its people and has decided to step down and join the ARP party. You will soon witness a tula daan to ensure the gods bless and guide him in this journey."

There was a thunderous applause.

"You must wonder if this old man has gone senile; I can't possibly work forever. Who will take over after I retire?" he continued. "I am pleased to announce that Surya, my grandson, will succeed me. He has all the qualities required to lead this company. He will be the youngest CEO in the history of corporate India. But this is not all; I have even better news! SGI has also bagged a telecom license; that's another project Surya will spearhead."

With love and gratitude gushing out from his heart, Surya hugged his grandfather amidst the cheer and jubilation.

Chana looked at Ashok for any indication of vexation. He had just been bypassed like a lousy artery that could no longer pump blood, but he looked as serene as the Buddha. Sharda's arms were tightly wrapped around Surya, and her tears flowed freely. It was evident she preferred being the 'mother of the king' rather than a 'wife of the prince in waiting'.

Surya mingled with the guests and continued to collect blessings. After embracing the Mumbai Commissioner of Police, Mr Prakash Yadav, he greeted Sethji Tulsidas Tekchand, the owner of CFC – SGI's biggest competitor in confectionery – and touched his feet. The Tekchands and the Jains maintained a cordial relationship in public while trying to disembowel each other in private. Sethji blessed him, murmuring the Sanskrit words meant for attaining eternal success: *yashasvi bhava*. Chana wondered how much sincerity Sethji loaded into that blessing before shooting it from his lips.

Finally, the main puja commenced. Ashok sat on one side of the gilded scale, and the chanting began with MJ making the first offering. The balancing of the scales went on for a while. After pretending to be self-denying, the scale eventually buckled under the weight of the fortune, hoisting Ashok in mid-air and finally landing with the riches on the other side with a thud.

Chana was impressed with Sharda's estimating abilities. The deal was finalised at a little over seventy kilos.

In the SGI office at Imperial Towers I, feeling languorous after the heavy meal, Chana loosened the drawstrings of her slacks and opened her desk drawer. She pulled out the invitation card that had been left behind.

Growing up in Italy, but on a diet rich in Hindi movies, Chana and her family were Bollywood-crazy. At seventeen years of age, Chana had arrived in Mumbai for her big break. Living in shoddy PG accommodations, she had enrolled for the entire package – song, dance, dialogue, and diction classes. Her transformation after one year was so phenomenal that nobody could guess that she was not a native of the land. Chana was ready to take over Bollywood. At her first meeting with a particular producer, she immediately understood what was expected of her and she was more than willing to comply. But after a few soft porn videos, nothing changed except that she became the sixty-five-year-old producer's mistress. Chana realised that her life was slipping through her fingers. She gave up on her Bollywood dream, started working as a receptionist, and worked her way up until she became MJ's PA at SGI. The producer's invitation card had to stay behind.

Chapter 4
Hasan

Hasan woke up startled. With clammy hands, he tried to separate his PJs that were clinging to his legs. The stench of urine hit him hard. He frantically peeled the covers off the mattress as he realised another nightmare had punctured his sleep.

Looking out of his bedroom door, Hasan noticed dead bodies relaxing in the living room.

He figured that the morning yoga class was in session. *Abu* was teaching his students how to loosen bodily and mental tension through the corpse posture – apparently a thing to achieve whilst still being alive, nowadays. Possessing the agility of a Boa constrictor, it was as if his father had been waiting at the threshold of this yoga-obsessed era for the world to finally take notice of his abilities.

The fleeting feeling of warmth towards his Abu passed, and his mind was volatile again; he reached for a *beedi* and tried to make sense of what had happened. Surely, something must have compelled his body to react in this manner. Were the old ghosts he thought he had fought off surfacing again? He vaguely remembered screaming at Salma, his ex-wife in the dream. But he had never raised his voice at her. Or had he?

Hasan checked his phone; it was Tuesday. Tuesdays meant sessions with his therapist. Another sham that the department was paying for him to connect with his 'inner

13

feelings'. But today's session would be exciting. He wanted to see the shock on the doctor's face when he relayed this little accident to him. Maybe Dr Poonawala could look down at his imaginary crystal ball and throw some light on this wet occurrence that had surfaced after many years.

In the kitchen, he reheated the tea that Abu had prepared for him in the microwave. A thin film appeared on top of the milky liquid. He hated microwaved tea. At the headquarters, the tea served by Anil from his street-side stall was always piping hot. The *cutting*, sweetened strong brew brought morsels of conversations with the other officers and the constables. He missed the action. Since his suspension two years ago, he had not had endorphins run madly in his bloodstream.

He had barely finished the tea when his phone beeped. It was a WhatsApp message from his boss. He stared at it for a long time in disbelief.

It said, *Report to duty immediately.*

Chapter 5
Shreyas

Mumbai, 17th June 2016

The translucent crescent of the onion was about to caress the curry leaf when a pockmarked wooden spoon forced them apart. The chilli hissed and spewed its venom, and Shreyas was suddenly reminded of his mother. He added an extra pod of garlic that retaliated with its pungent odour. Turning up the flame, Shreyas wiped the beads of sweat off his forehead, wondering how his pregnant wife usually cooked in this heat.

"Do you need help?" Savita's voice boomed from the bedroom. Living in a 500-square-foot matchbox, the speed of sound was hardly an issue.

"No, I can handle it," he replied.

"I think it is done," she said from the doorway. Her enormous belly still shocked him every time he saw it.

"Why did you get up? I can make my own *dabba*."

"*Aai* will be home any moment. What will she think if she sees her darling son cooking and her daughter-in-law in bed?"

"I don't care; you need to rest."

She waddled back into the living room while Shreyas spooned the poha into his tiffin box.

"I think Vijay is a lovely name. It was Amitabh Bachchan's name in a lot of the cop movies. If it's a baby girl, we can call her Vijaya," Savita spoke, her nose buried in a film magazine. "Boy or girl, it will be a *wardiwala*'s kid, haan?" she continued.

15

"We will name him Ranveer, after my favourite actor," Shivu, Shreyas's fifteen-year-old brother, chimed in.

"Stop watching so many movies and concentrate on your studies. You have to become a big man," his bhabhi admonished.

"That sounds like a lot of work; I will do what my *baba* did – run a *paan* shop, drink *tharra* and watch movies all day!" Shivu chuckled.

"Shut up, silly boy," his brother said, laughing it off.

"If it's a boy, I am going to name him Yuvraj, after my favourite cricketer, and if it's a girl, then whatever you want," Shreyas said, smiling at his wife. "But I have got my first big case, so I think it is a girl. Girls are supposed to be lucky for their fathers," he added.

Two years ago, when Shreyas had met Savita, she was the most sought-after stylist at the 'Woke Hair' salon. Her hair, shiny and luscious, was full of life. Today, her hair, dry and frizzy, was taunting him with its dullness. He desperately needed a lucky break to catapult his career.

"This Surya Jain death case – you think he was murdered?" Savita enquired, bringing him back to the present.

"Nothing can be said until the investigation is over."

"Who has been assigned that case?"

"There is a rumour that Crime Branch Officer Hasan has been called back."

"Why didn't you tell me! Isn't he your idol?" Savita was surprised.

"Yes," he replied, somewhat embarrassed. "Anyway, I must head out now."

Savita added two laddoos to his steel dabba. She intuitively knew that it was going to be a late night for him.

Chapter 6
Urvashi

Mumbai, 17th June 2016

Arms firmly placed on the handles, the driver twisted his upper body for a sharp left turn before pulling the brakes and bringing the rickshaw to an abrupt halt. Fixing his hair in the rear-view mirror, he extended his other hand, palm open, to collect the fare.

Urvashi shoved his hand out of her way as she squirmed herself out of the seat.

Surprised by the arrogance, the driver glanced over his shoulder, and on the first sighting of the officious police uniform, his lower lip began to quiver as if she had caught him red-handed.

From the bevy of reactions that came her way: kowtowing, fear, anticipation, it was *fear* that Urvashi loved the most. The manner in which the hoi polloi shuddered when they saw her in uniform. The reaction was the only good part of her job. She hated everything else.

It had not been her dream to join the IPS; it had been transferred onto her by her father. All Urvashi had ever wanted was to get married and settle down. She had heard her father say jokingly to his friends, "With her stern demeanour, marriage will always be a hit and a miss, but she will surely be successful in the police force."

With her big build, Urvashi knew she was nothing like her three sisters. All of them were slender, gentle, and

17

'made to order' to match the matrimonial descriptions in the newspapers. True to form, they all had flown off the matrimonial shelves like freshly baked bread.

But what annoyed her the most was when it was time for her father to look for a suitable match for her, he had not tried hard enough. There was no hurry, he said. But time was slipping away, and all this waiting was making her bitter.

She noticed a young couple walk ahead. They had their fingers intertwined. From the back, Urvashi could see the woman's big ass jiggle as she leaned trustfully into her partner.

Urvashi sucked her stomach in and quickly picked up her pace. She *had* to see how the woman looked. Was she prettier than her?

Hurrying ahead, she crossed the road and casually looked in the couple's direction. Definitely not attractive. She hated attractive women, but she hated unattractive women who were married even more.

Arching her back straight, she crossed the road again, and walked imperiously towards the couple. Immediately, the couple separated their hands. She had got the desired reaction without uttering a word.

Her phone rang. It was her father.

"Have you reached?" his voice demanded impatiently.

"Not yet, I still have to take the train. Is *he* there already?"

"Yes."

"Is your news confirmed?" she asked in a hushed tone.

"Unfortunately, it is correct," her father responded, sighing heavily. "You may be the inspector, and you may continue to think of my colleagues and me as old *pandu hawaldars*, but our network is secure, and our connections run deep."

"I know, Baba."

"You should have been there by now. The media is covering everything "

"Let me take a cab then," she hung up hurriedly. She was getting tired of him micro-managing her life.

As much as she hated to admit it, Baba was right. She couldn't afford to be late for this one.

Forty minutes later, Urvashi disembarked from her cab and saw Hasan almost immediately. He was standing across the Sansani News' TV reporter. Of standard height, he was wearing a dull white shirt with a rebellious button threatening to burst open and worn-out leather sandals that were left unslung at the rear. His long-nailed fingers were peeling a banana as he smiled widely at the TV correspondent.

To Urvashi, Crime Branch Officer Hasan, with his belly that reeked of middle-class aspirations, looked like the very hallmark of 'average'. Before his fall from grace, Hasan had enjoyed a formidable reputation and had been hailed as one of the only officers to have come up the ranks so quickly. She had been apprehensive about working with him. But this chubby-tubby image put her at ease instantly. As she got closer, she noticed that the anchor's performance had so consumed him that he hadn't realized that his hands were peeling the banana upside down. A smirk escaped her lips.

Chapter 7
Imperial Towers I

Mumbai, 17th June 2016

After forty minutes of decrypting a whirlwind of faces, Shreyas spotted the Inspector insignia proudly gleaming in the morning sun. Stubbing his beedi, he rushed towards her.

"Hello, Urvashi ma'am? I am Sub-Inspector Shreyas," he saluted her. "So good to finally meet you, Madam."

Urvashi nodded distractedly.

"Just waiting for Hasan sir," he continued. "I am so excited to meet both of you on the same day."

"He is here already," she said, pointing towards him.

"Who? That... that man peeling the banana the wrong way?" Shreyas asked, bewildered. He had heard stories about officer Hasan's non-conformism, but this was outright comical.

"Yes."

Jostling through the crowds, they made their way towards Hasan. "Hello Sir, I am Sub-Inspector Shreyas," he saluted again, somewhat dejectedly, "and this is Urvashi ma'am."

"*I* am the Station House Officer and *my* station got a call that Surya Jain was found dead," Urvashi spoke with authority.

"Oh, hello!" Hasan responded cheerfully.

"You are peeling it the wrong way," Urvashi pointed at the banana with a raised eyebrow.

"What?" Hasan asked with his mouth full.

"The *banana*," she spoke slowly, as if speaking to a child.

"Ah, that is herd stupidity, to do what others do, without thinking," he declared. "Have you ever seen a chimpanzee eat a banana, Urvashi?"

"What?" she asked, confused.

"Simple question really, have you ever seen a chimpanzee eat a banana? This is how they peel it. The stem actually makes for a nice handle. Nature provided for it, as it provided for nails to dig deep into an orange peel, and still, most humans do it wrong. You should visit the zoo often. You will learn the most efficient way of eating fruit."

"Let's go in," Urvashi said, looking at him with disgust.

Equipped with their IDs, they made their way through the security towards the only operational elevator in Imperial Towers I. The area outside the lobby was bustling with well-dressed executives heaving themselves around.

"SGI lobby?" the liftman enquired, hoping to overhear what the police had to say about the case.

"Yes," Shreyas responded.

"Who found the body?" Hasan asked.

"The cleaner," Urvashi replied. "I have asked him to be held back for an interrogation."

"What is the estimated time of death?"

"It was between 8 and 9 p.m. last night, but since he fell on the ledge of the 23rd floor and not on the street, nobody found the body till morning."

"This is exclusively an office tower, right?" Hasan added.

"Yes," Urvashi responded. "Everyone needs an ID to enter the building and to operate the elevators. SGI offices are on the 49th and 50th floors. The tower has a CCTV camera at the entrance and in the parking. Another entrance connects the 48th floor with a retail complex, for which one also needs an access card. Surya came in the late afternoon and did not leave the building. SGI uses the services of a company called

The Urban Planters for the maintenance of their indoor and outdoor plants. The gardening team came in to water the plants at about six in the morning, as usual. Their finger and footprints are all over the place. Surya's phone is also smashed, and there are no signs of a scuffle," she added.

"Is there a CCTV at the retail complex entrance?" Hasan asked.

"There is, sir, but the camera broke many months ago," the liftman interjected. "Nobody got it fixed," he continued.

Shreyas realised that it was no longer the barbers or the secretaries, but the liftmen of multi-floor corporates that were today's talebearers. They were invisible to the people, but their eyes saw everything, even things behind their backs.

The elevator announced the arrival of their destination with a ding.

Marble floors and grey walls defined the reception of SGI. A few plush velvet chairs were peppered around a large TV that seamlessly blended with the back wall.

An attractive woman scampered across in her stilettos. "Hi, I am Chana, MJ's PA. Can I help you?"

"We are investigating Surya's death, and we would like to ask you a few questions," Hasan said, handing out his ID.

"Sure," she replied.

"How many people work in this office?" Urvashi asked.

"About sixty in this office. It is the headquarters of our Foods division; we have Saachi Chocolates and Saachi Milk operating from here."

"Tell us about yesterday; what happened in the office?" Urvashi asked.

"It was a relaxed day as the bosses had a big religious event at their home. They came to work only around 5 p.m."

"What happened after that?"

"There was a 5 p.m. meeting in the conference room here with our Japanese partners."

"And after that?"

"As I said, it was light at work. My boss, MJ, left at 6:30 p.m., and I left shortly after."

"What was Surya doing at that time?" Hasan probed.

"I have no idea; his office is on another floor."

"You didn't see him at all?"

"He did come down to this floor once, but then he went back up."

"How were his relations with you?"

"They were fine."

"Did he have any enemies in the office?" Urvashi quizzed her.

"Enemies, no, but he didn't get along with Mishal."

"Who is Mishal?" Urvashi asked.

"He is the Marketing Manager of A1 Chocolates. Let me buzz him in," Chana said, jamming a few buttons on the intercom.

"Does only Surya's office have a terrace?" Hasan asked.

"Yes, he loved the terrace; it helped him unwind after work."

"Unwind how?" Hasan persisted.

Chana hesitated before speaking, "I will tell you, but please don't quote me. He used to snort coke out there."

"Aren't all the Jains teetotallers and all of that?" Hasan said, confused.

"Yes, in public. Anyway, cocaine is not alcohol, sir," Chana answered sincerely.

"So this clearly is just a case of overdose," Urvashi surmised.

They were interrupted by a dapper-looking man dressed in a crisp white shirt and slim-fit trousers.

"Hello, I am Mishal Mishra."

"Hello, you seem to be the villain of this story," Hasan said.

"No surprises there. Unfortunately, I never got along with Surya, and everyone in the office knew that."

"So that's why you killed him?" Hasan said.

"Then a lot more people from the company would have been dead," Mishal said matter-of-factly.

"So you don't like a lot of people working here?" Urvashi reconfirmed.

"Yes," he said, glancing at Chana.

"What do you do in the company?" Urvashi asked.

"I am the Marketing Manager of A1, the original SGI chocolate brand. A few years ago, when Surya joined the family business, the pretty boy needed a new toy to play with, so SGI hired Megh as the New Product Technologist and Ali as the Manufacturing guy. The trio worked together to create a chocolate called D'sire. That brand won many awards. But around six to eight months after its launch, the product was discontinued as it was embroiled in a controversy for having traces of ADR. I had suspected something was off and had even tried to get the attention of the senior management, but nobody cared at the time."

"What is ADR?" Hasan asked.

"Animal-derived Rennet is a coagulating enzyme that's obtained from the stomachs of baby calves, usually obtained by killing them. It was bad news for SGI," he added.

"Why is that?" Urvashi asked.

"Madam, the Indian consumer believes that anything that is vegetarian or Ayurvedic is superior to anything that doesn't tout that claim. SGI has built an entire empire playing on that psyche of the Vedic obsessed in India. Having traces of ADR is terrible news for a company whose USP is that they are 100% vegetarian."

"What happened after that?" Urvashi asked.

"They discontinued the brand. Now they are back to manufacturing only A1 Chocolates."

"Did they find out who was responsible?" Urvashi asked.

"Yes, there was an internal investigation that revealed that it was my boss, Toni Mehta, MJ's son-in-law and the head of A1 Chocolates, who was responsible."

"Why would he do that?" Hasan asked.

"To ensure that D'sire failed and only his chocolate – A1 – remained in the race. Family rivalry is complicated."

"Were you party to this?" Hasan asked.

"Absolutely not."

"Was he tried in court?"

"No, when this news broke out in the media, he was in Karnataka at our milk factory. It was around the same time as the violent cow vigilante incidents. The public was already infuriated, and sentiments were raging high. He was mob lynched, and he died."

"So, after D'sire was discontinued, what was Surya's role in the business?"

"He became my boss."

"And you both still fought?"

"No, I can't fight with my boss. But yes, I was not too fond of him."

"When did you last see him?" Urvashi asked.

"I saw him on the day he died. I worked on the presentation for our Japanese partners all morning, and he showed up at 5 p.m. and presented it."

"And what time did you leave?"

"I left at 6:30 p.m. after the presentation was done."

"What was Surya doing then?"

"The presentation went very well. He was informed immediately that SGI had bagged the project. He was ecstatic. He had already poured his first drink. Usually, it was a long night when he did that, as he wanted to finish his quota in the office."

"What do you think this was: a suicide, a murder, or an accident?" Urvashi prodded him further.

"Suicide is most unlikely; accident is most likely, but I wouldn't rule out murder. Surya was a bastard and had rubbed many people the wrong way, especially since the D'sire scandal. Megh, Ali or anyone could have wanted it."

"But that was a long time ago," Urvashi said dismissively. "Who else interacted with Surya regularly?"

"Roma, his PA. I will ask her to come right away," Chana chipped in.

"Can I go now?" Mishal asked.

"One last question before you leave. Why did you suspect, 'something was off'?" Hasan asked.

"I don't know if you ever ate D'sire, but it was a bloody good, competitively-priced chocolate with an unmatchable silkiness which is only possible when you use very good quality cocoa. Our company is not very generous with our raw materials. It had to have something else that they were not disclosing."

"That's what you thought! Did anyone else feel that way?" Urvashi enquired.

Shreyas caught Chana cross her arms across her chest and stare at Mishal in defiance.

"No," he answered. "Can I go now?"

"Yes, but don't leave the city," Hasan added as he hurried out.

"Hello, I am Roma, Surya's PA. May I come in?" a small voice said from the door.

"Please take a seat," Hasan said.

"How could this happen to him? He was a gentleman," Roma said, comforting her watery kohl-smudged eyes with a lace handkerchief.

"Really? Many seem to agree that he was a bastard," Hasan remarked.

"One must not talk like that about the dead!"

"Why not? Do all bastards become saints as soon as they die?" Hasan quipped.

That was a question that Shreyas had been asking himself since his father died. Every year, his mother made all of them fast for the peace of mind of his dead father. In offering gratitude to someone who was both alcoholic and abusive, his mother denied food to the sober and the respectful who were alive.

"Tell me Roma darling," Hasan continued. "About this gentleman of yours. Did you sleep with him?" Hasan asked casually.

"How dare you ask me that!" Roma exclaimed.

"Just answer the question."

"No, I did not sleep with him."

Urvashi chipped in, "Did you find anything out of the ordinary these last few days?"

Roma fidgeted momentarily with her lace handkerchief and replied, "Well, yesterday, when I was setting up the boardroom for the presentation, I heard loud noises from MJ sir's office. I noticed through his glass door that he was yelling at Ashok sir. I immediately buzzed Surya, who went straight into MJ sir's office and got caught up in the argument."

"What was the argument about?"

"I don't know. I could only see their expressions through the glass door, but not hear their conversation."

"Was Surya in a serious relationship with anyone?"

"Many girls kept coming and going out of his life, but nothing serious."

"Any friends?"

Roma said sympathetically, "He didn't have many. A lot of the ones he thought were his friends used to call to borrow money or ask for favours, so he kept his distance."

"Who did he meet during the past week?" Hasan asked.

"I don't remember all at the top of my head, but one meeting was with an acquaintance who pitched a new business idea, and the other, with a friend who invited him to her wedding," she said.

"Send me a list of all the people he met, in and out of the office," Hasan finished.

"Yes. Can I go now?"

"Yes!"

"Sir, the window cleaner who found the dead body is waiting to give his statement," Chana said.

"Let's meet him. Who identified the body on behalf of the family?" Hasan asked Chana.

"MJ, poor man, he was very shaken; he suffered a minor attack. It is not easy to see your grandson's body like that."

They were led to a conference room where a frail man was seated wearing the cleaning company's uniform.

"What is your name?" Urvashi asked.

"Ajay Tiwari."

"Tell us what you saw," Urvashi said sternly.

"This morning, I came to work as usual. I was cleaning the window on the twenty-third floor when I saw something outside. When I went to check, I saw a leg and then the body," he broke down.

"Can you take us to Surya's office?" Urvashi said to Chana who was trying to calm the cleaner.

"Can you hurry up?" Urvashi snapped.

"Yes, of course," Chana hastened and led them through the reception, where the mammoth TV was covering the story from inside Zanara.

"Isn't that Amit Sehgal from that reality show?" Hasan remarked, pointing to the screen, his face giddy with excitement. "I absolutely love him!" Within moments, he had kicked off his sandals and was sitting cross-legged opposite the TV.

"Hasan, we have to go to the fiftieth floor," Urvashi said, her lips tightly pressed.

"Na, I am not interested! The forensics team does a better job with the dead. We'll do better in the company of the alive. And I would rather watch this," he said, nodding at the TV. "See, it's Karan Singh, the famous singer, entering their house! You guys better hurry up so that we can rush to Zanara. I don't want to miss out on all the action," he continued. "And one more thing, tell the forensics lab that I want a complete toxicology report. I want to know each and every drug Surya had indulged in!" With that, he leaned back and made himself comfortable on the plush velvet chair.

The onscreen reporters were obsessing over the entry of yet another superstar in Zanara when Hasan's phone rang. It was the Commissioner of Police, Prakash Yadav. The call reminded him why he hated these high-profile cases. There was always someone meddling in the investigation.

"Hello, my man; good to have you back," the commissioner said.

"Good to be back, sir."

"This Surya Jain's death looks like an open and shut case; surely an accident, it's a waste of your valuable time."

"Hardly sir, it is a sudden death, most unnatural. We must wait for a detailed report."

"But that will take some time," the commissioner egged on.

"Sir, I don't know how to hurry the dead and make them cooperate."

The commissioner hesitated before speaking, "The family, as you can imagine, want the body quickly. They are sure it's an accident and do not suspect any foul play."

"Very kind of them, sir," Hasan said sarcastically.

"Poor MJ, he doesn't want the world to know that his grandson was well, an occasional abuser."

"Junkie is more like it, sir. His people tell me that he abused most drugs, including coke and ecstasy," Hasan said.

"That's precisely the kind of information the Jains don't want smeared across the media," the commissioner said. "So, I'd be very careful if I were you, Hasan. You don't need excessive public interest, especially on your first case back."

"I assure you I will be careful, sir," Hasan said before hanging up.

Chapter 8
Aadi

London, 17th June 2016

"Hot towel, sir?" the attendant hovered around him. Zipping up his pants, Aadi took the towel from the man and handed him the customary twenty-pound note. Looking in the mirror, he detected a greying patch on his chin. Not usually self-absorbed, he felt cheated today by its sudden appearance. Still staring at himself, he flashed his ebullient boyish smile and witnessed years chip away from his face. His confidence reinstated, he stepped into the lounge that welcomed him with the familiar gentle clinking of glasses.

Waiting for his flight, he sipped his wine from a special stemmed Waterford and nibbled on a piece of brie from the platter laid out for him.

"Your flight has almost finished boarding. Can I serve you anything else, sir?" a sweet looking airline staff asked.

"Nothing else, thanks," Aadi replied, flashing his boyish smile once again. He looked around. It was the usual business crowd, but today amongst them, a family was traveling upper class for the first time; their kids were running around excitedly. Some regular travellers had a look of disapproval, but not Aadi; the airline's first-class lounge was his sanctum sanctorum. Here, he was unflustered by the sounds of everyday life.

At that moment, he caught sight of the rolling ticker on the TV.

Surya Jain, the heir of Saachi Group International found dead!
Darting towards the TV, he dialled up the volume, and it boomed loudly: *The corporate world bleeds… quite literally! This morning, the dead body of Surya Jain, the prince of the SGI group, was found on the ledge of the twenty-third floor of Imperial Towers I. He fell from the terrace of his office on the fiftieth floor of the same building. Police have begun investigations. More details awaited.*

The newsreader faded out, and in the absence of a live feed, a hackneyed online picture of Imperial Towers I took centre stage with a comical illustration of a man lying in a pool of blood, whose heart, ironically, was steadily pumping on screen.

"Sir, is everything all right? The flight has already boarded. They are just waiting for you," the hostess persisted.

Aadi didn't respond. Wildly punching 'Wifey' on his phone, he whizzed out of the lounge in a tearing hurry to get back home. Aboard the plane, he jammed a few other numbers, but no one answered.

After great reluctance, he called Rambo.

Chapter 9
Rambo

There is a new Willy Wonka in town.
Exactly a year ago, Seth Tulsidas Tekchand, the CEO of Consolidated Foodstuff Company (CFC) moved his company headquarters from Malta to Mumbai. Their brands were already popular in half the world when the business tycoon announced they were diversifying aggressively and would be setting up a chocolate factory in India. Their debutante brand, shrouded in mystery and touted to be the belle of the ball, would be locking horns with established players such as Cadbury and SGI for a piece of the lion's share. Though Sethji (as he prefers to be addressed) started the empire, his son Rammeher Tekchand, better known as Rambo, is managing the reins today. In an exclusive interview with AR News, Rambo will share his plans for the best-kept secret in the world of chocolate engineering. We will also be asking this eligible groom about his much-hyped wedding to the Greek goddess Avanti, his cricket team Mumbai Musketeers, and his unique gift - his memory.

Rambo looked at the picture inserted in this article. His eyes appeared magnified, making him look like an impala caught off guard by the headlights of the safari. He felt like one too. The interview mentioned in the article was scheduled for today. No matter what Sethji said, Rambo knew that this interview would be very different from their dog and pony show of Malta.

In Malta, Sethji always had the same tricks, and the questions followed a pattern.

"Everyone, I want you to meet my son Rambo. He is a genius, really. I don't want you to believe me just because I am saying it; I am going to prove it to you," he would say, beaming with pride.

The first question was always about the stock prices of various FMCG companies in a given year; Rambo would answer in less than a minute. But he was not a one-trick pony; he could do many. The questions would become progressively more difficult, all the time testing his eidetic memory. *"The Malta prime minister is proud of you"*, Sethji would say at the end. That comment always made Rambo very happy. It assured him that in Malta, despite his quirks, he would always be valued as a national treasure. But here in Mumbai, nobody could depend on yesterday's tricks; it was a city of today and now. You had to earn your applause each day.

Eliza had prepped him well. They had gone over every detail for hours, but the reporters were notorious for trespassing into prohibited territory, and asking questions that were not a part of the script, and he was infamous for being dumbstruck. His social ineptness flared up under the spotlight. When a stranger asked him something, even if he knew the answers in his heart, he could not get himself to utter them.

Rambo hoped for a distraction. After that horrible incident at Imperial Towers I, he had expected a lockdown of the entire complex, but the police had only cordoned off Tower I. At Imperial Towers II, it was business as usual.

Rambo looked at this watch. The reporter would be here in an hour. He stared at Sethji and felt a cold shiver run down his spine. He tried to fathom why he, a thirty-year-old man, was still so terrorised by his father's presence. Sethji was leaning majestically over his cassata green and pink conference table, a piece executed in Bhiwandi Furniture Market, but introduced to the world as a progeny of Italian ancestry, and was delivering a presentation in the boardroom when the distraction happened.

Rambo had prayed for it, but had not expected the universe to respond with such a catastrophic event. His phone started to ring; something that never happened — because nobody called him. Nobody.

The caller ID flashed the name 'Aadi'. Rambo's bulbous eyeballs bulged even more.

Rammeher Tekchand, the sole heir of CFC, wondered why he felt this constricted in Aadi's presence. Aadi's charm *was* effortless and all-pervasive; on many occasions, he had witnessed Mumbai's pennies and diamonds scamper to schmooze Aadi. It was as if they were honoured that he let them hover around him. Sethji, on the other hand, could only manage to buy a thin veneer of loyalty for his money. It was only natural, he convinced himself, that he too, was tongue-tied by Aadi's magnetism. After all, Aadi was Avanti's brother, his brother-in-law. *Almost* his brother-in-law.

"Who is it?" Sethji's stern voice interrupted his trance.

Suddenly the boardroom started spinning. The ringtone picked up momentum. Rambo saw a slender arm reach out for the phone from behind him. He wanted to stop the arm, wring it and dislodge it from its shoulder before it got to the phone, but he helplessly watched as it lowered its flawlessly manicured digits and picked up the instrument.

"Hello," she murmured into the phone in her usual calm voice. "It's Eliza."

The room stood still.

"Rambo is in a board meeting and cannot be reached," she spoke confidently.

As she continued to listen to the caller intently, Rambo detected a frown kneeling on all fours on her gleaming forehead.

"I will look into it at the earliest," she said before hanging up.

Rambo sensed Sethji's biting glare pierce through Eliza's translucent face, but she shot a look that said *It's nothing important, let's continue* at him with her unblinking eyes. Sethji faced the whiteboard again.

Rambo's bulbous eyes returned to their sockets. Peace was restored.

Chapter 10
Sethji

From the corner of his eyes, Sethji watched Eliza stealthily slip out of the room. As much as he detested her camaraderie with Rambo, he was absolutely in awe of her resourcefulness.

As soon as he had heard about Surya Jain's death, Sethji knew that Rambo would receive a call and wouldn't know how to handle it. Even now, he was cowering behind the Finance Manager.

Sethji's mind was racing to find out about the caller. He was sure that the caller was Aadi, but he would have to wait until this damned meeting was over to find out. It was a terrible thing to happen to any family, to lose their heir, but then, as they say, Karma is a bitch.

He could not wait to read the headlines. He hoped that the post-mortem report cited drug and alcohol overdose as the cause of Surya's death; the world would finally get to see the real face of the Jains.

On the wall facing him, almost side-lined by the certifications and licences, hung a framed picture of an almond-eyed, zestful girl bearing a striking resemblance to his wife. A younger and prettier version of her. Only it was not her; it was Reema – his first-born. His heart ached with fresh pain.

Chapter 11
Eliza

Mumbai, 17th June 2016

Eliza looked at her watch; it had been one hour since Aadi's call. She knew that he would call again. Visualising the office's blueprint, she was sure that she had checked everywhere and had asked everyone in the office about Megh, but nobody seemed to know about her whereabouts.

What if Megh was dead? Would it be better that way?

Her body shivered at the thought. *Was* it normal for people to think or even wish for people to be dead? She didn't particularly hate Megh, not as much as she hated Avanti, but she didn't like her either. Maybe if Megh was dead, Rambo's wedding with Avanti would be called off. That would give Rambo some time to figure out that it was Eliza, who he actually loved. Suddenly she remembered the one place that she hadn't checked yet.

Sprinting through the hallway, she hit M on the elevator and started prepping like a surgeon preparing for surgery. Tying her hair in a bun, she pulled out her pack of wipes and surgically removed the make-up from her face. Next, she took off all her jewellery, and finally, she unclasped her Cartier watch and threw it in her bag.

On the Mezzanine level, she surrendered her bag and traded in her tweed Chanel jacket for a white lab coat and her Gucci shoes for the industrial socks. Battling the strong chemical stench, she marched towards the lab. Eliza was unable to comprehend why any woman would want to work in such a setting.

Adjusting to the white light, her eyes scanned the lab and zoned in on a silhouette behind a glass door. A form more feminine than the others was holding a giant hammer in one hand. Suddenly, with a jolt, the hammer struck, shattering something into a million little pieces that went flying across the room. Eliza found herself amidst loud cheering as she walked through the door. Megh was holding the hammer high above her head.

Unenlightened about the search party on her lookout, Megh said jubilantly, "Eliza, you must try my latest innovation, crispy monster chips! They scored the highest on the crispness test."

"Where is your phone?" Eliza retorted curtly.

"In my bag. Why?"

"When did you last check it?"

"Not in a while. What's wrong?"

"Call Aadi," she commanded.

Megh's look of confusion thrilled her. She felt a rush of malicious pleasure in knowing that this time, the brave and bold Megh was dependent on her for information. Eliza started walking away, almost certain that Megh would call her name.

"Eliza, wait!"

She smiled and turned around, but it was not Megh. It was Dr Janardhan, the chief scientist at CFC Labs. She was holding a cardboard box and grinning widely.

"Eliza, let me introduce you to Rambo's new skin! The thinnest glove ever manufactured that mimics the feel and the look of human skin. I had done many fittings with Rambo, and he had been okay with the last two models, but I wasn't satisfied, so I did some more work and have produced this," she said, excitedly shoving the box in her hand. "When Rambo slips it on, even he won't know the difference. Now he doesn't need to worry about shaking hands with so many people at his wedding. Please give it to him."

Eliza's face turned pale. Rambo's marriage was increasingly becoming a reality.

Chapter 12
Megh

Out of her frozen lab and in the open car park, Megh hurried in the direction of her sanctum: the smokers' corner. Right in front of her, in a quiet and deserted plot of commercial Mumbai was the half-constructed Namaste Tower in the shape of the Indian greeting. With another recession pounding the construction sector with its invisible hammer, what was to be a structure equivalent and consummate of Indian values and ideology, now stood lacklustre and incomplete.

A hammer was in her hands that morning when she conducted the crispy and crunchy test on her German snap and bend machine. The crunchy meter registered responses as one of the three possibilities: Too much, ideal, or insufficient. Each chip though identical in shape and size, uttered a different cry when struck.

A hammer was over her head now, and its fall was imminent. She wondered how the machine would measure her cry for help. Too much, ideal, or insufficient?

She looked around; her fellow corporate smokers were smoking and murmuring amidst themselves; their speculations about Surya's death were more chilling than her lab's air conditioning. Finishing her cigarette, she rushed towards her car and called Aadi.

"Megh! Where the fuck have you been?" he hollered.

"I am so sorry, but I was in the lab. Please don't yell at me, I am panicking as is!"

Aadi's voice softened, "I am sorry; I was just worried."

"How could he be dead?" she murmured.

"What do you think happened?"

"How would I know? Why would you ask me that question?"

"He was your boss; you knew him."

"In the past."

"Do you think it was a murder?"

"I don't know, Aadi, but they have the Crime Branch on it; they will surely dig D'sire, and then me."

"You have done nothing and have nothing to hide."

"I hadn't done anything even then; they still fired me."

"It's surely an accident. It will be sorted. Go home and relax."

"Okay."

"One last thing."

"What?"

"I love you."

There was a distinct pause. Her brain was screaming in her head. *Say I love you too*, but she couldn't get herself to do it.

"I have to go now," she said and hung up.

Chapter 13
MJ

Mumbai, 17th June 2016

MJ opened his eyes and took a few seconds to find his bearings. Thankfully, the room looked familiar. He was grateful that his family had not forgotten his instructions. No matter how critical, he wanted to be treated at home. Always.

He tried to get his mind to focus on the present, to make sense of the floating silhouettes in the room, but his past flashed in front of his eyes. He was reminded of when he was Motilal, and not MJ, and had started his journey in an oversized, borrowed suit from a small village in Chavad, Gujarat, to Dubai onboard the MV Dara, a passenger steamer. It was a short five-day journey, but the experience was deep-seated in his memory. Onboard, Motilal spent most days following Captain Saatchi of MV Dara and marvelling at his attributes as if he was a specimen to be admired and feared at the same time.

Always dressed in his pristine white uniform, the Captain knew how to regale the passengers with his easy laughter, and discipline the crew with his imposing personality. Motilal aspired to be like the white man in white clothing. The ship finally made it safely to the shores of Dubai. Disembarking, Motilal felt the desert immediately. It was as if the sun had been mounted on top of a pedestal fan and was hitting him steadily with the warm Sirocco wind that blew sand in his eyes. He had barely managed to wash the sand grains out of his hair, when three days later, a bomb exploded, and MV Dara sunk to the depths of the sea, taking Captain Saatchi and other crew members who were aboard the passenger liner with it.

In Chavad, Motilal was the son of a Brahmin, but in Dubai, he was a fabric assistant hired by a Gujarati textile shop owner whose referral system would put modern social networking sites to shame. Furling fabric spools in the textile shop by the Dubai Creek, it dawned upon Motilal that he was unfurling the days, months, and years of his life. He was restless; he missed India and wanted to go back, quick and rich.

On many occasions, he had spotted His Highness, the Sheikh, sip *kava* and engage with the Indian trading community, but it took him two years to approach him for a trade license decree for his own company. His Highness smiled, handed him the paper napkin that accompanied his kava, and told him to write the name of his new outfit. Motilal's fingers trembled when he slowly wrote in English *Saachi* (truth). Paying tribute to his hero, the Captain, the slight alteration in the spelling let him ride on the back of purity, honesty, and truthfulness to build his image. Motilal morphed into MJ.

A voice was calling out to him, reverberating from afar. It was Bhanu, she was talking to him slowly. He saw her gentle face, but it did not bear her trademark smile. The sinking feeling hit him like a lashing tide.

Surya was dead.

A phone rang, spurring activity in the room. Ashok answered it. The caller said something, prompting Ashok's pitch to surge in response.

That idiot Ashok, he can never hide his thoughts, MJ thought to himself. Then with great difficulty, he gesticulated for the phone and asked for it to be held to his ear.

"Hello," his voice was barely a whisper.

"The police are on their way to your house. Senior Inspector Hasan from the Crime Branch has also been appointed on the case."

The jagged voice on the other end continued, "His last case was that Bollywood actress' death. Poor guy; there were rumours that his wife ran away with his best friend, and that messed him up. He said and did all the wrong things. He was suspended. This is his first case after that. Nothing to worry. We will control the report. He is quite a joker, though the lady officer is someone to look out for. Too sharp."

Chapter 14
Shreyas

Mumbai, 17th June 2016

As a Sub-Inspector, most of Shreyas' professional life had been about hunting down petty criminals: the derelict, the destitute, and the desperate. But for the first time, he was working on a case where the laws of the land were ruled by the wealthy, well-heeled and well-provided for. This land was foreign to him.

In his *chawl*, the news that he was a part of the high-profile Surya Jain case had spread like wildfire, and his neighbours spoke to him with a new-found deference that really stroked his ego. He was determined to succeed.

Shreyas noticed a stream of commoners and nobles entering the palatial lobby as Vilas, the constable, steered their car into the one-way road that led to Zanara's driveway.

"Hello sir, Pandya Singh reporting on duty," a junior constable interjected their entry and saluted the trio, recognizing Hasan even though none of them were in uniform.

"Hello," responded Hasan. "I want you to be here 24/7. Keep a tab on everyone entering and leaving this house."

"Yes, sir."

"You asked for a constable? Without informing me?" Urvashi was livid.

"Are you upset because you didn't think of it or because you want us to play husband and wife? From today, we will share everything, okay darling?" Hasan smirked.

"Oh, I would never marry a loser like you!" she hollered.

In the living room, a sea of people wrapped in different hues of white were seated on thin foam mattresses. They were facing a large-framed picture of Surya at the front of the hall. A diamond crystal chandelier delicately dangled from the high ceiling while a wireless speaker surrendered itself to Jagjit Singh's soulful bhajans.

The police lined up beside a sheesham cabinet, next to a family portrait.

Shreyas pointed to a middle-aged man in the portrait. "That's Ashok, Surya's father. I have seen his pictures in the newspapers."

"And that's his sister, Bhanu Priya," Urvashi said, pointing to an unassuming lady wearing a salmon-coloured saree in the portrait. Standing in the second row, her face was barely visible inside the constructs of her tightly held pallu.

"Apparently, she had an affair with a Muslim student. Who would believe that looking at her simpleton image," she said sarcastically. "The affair cost her a college degree, though she was a college topper, and they got her married off early. Her late husband, Toni Mehta…" she continued, pointing to a handsome-looking fellow in the portrait, "was a womaniser," she said, sighing.

"Wasn't he the one who put that ADR stuff in D'sire?" Shreyas asked.

"Yes, it was Karma that he died. Trying to pollute our religion, that *dharambhrasht* man," Urvashi chastised.

"Poor Bhanu, she got married against her wishes, and then her husband turned out to be a scoundrel," Shreyas said empathetically.

"It's her fault. She should have known better than to have an affair with a Muslim," Urvashi declared, looking straight at Hasan in the eye.

"Bhanu now lives with them in Zanara, right?" Shreyas added quickly.

"Yes, Surya was apparently very fond of her and very protective of her son, Kabir," Urvashi finished.

"Kabir? Where was he when Surya died?" Hasan asked, his curiosity piqued.

"Studying at a university in America. He lands today. I have already checked his alibi," Urvashi added.

"How efficient! Did you check if he has a *Muslim* girlfriend at university?" he said sneeringly.

"Let's break up and mix around," Shreyas suggested as he tried to steer the conversation back on track.

The police blended in the crowd with pasted smiles and folded hands, and became party to the inner circle conversations and conspiracy theories.

Two old ladies, twinning in their traditional funeral wear, had conflicting reports: One was sure Surya had committed suicide because of the debt the Jains had accumulated over the years, and the other believed Surya was killed as he had fucked around with the mistress of a local goon.

Shreyas even learned about the Agarwal and Bhandari daughters. Both had hoped to marry Surya and were now brought together by their grief.

"Look, that's Mrs Raheja of Showtime Events," Sheetal Agarwal said, pointing to a lady wearing oversized glasses who walked by with an unchecked air of authority.

"She is friends with the Jains, but is not in the innermost circle yet. She is so desperate to make inroads with the Jains that she has decided to take over the event."

"Event? What event?" Shreyas enquired, innocently tapping Sheetal from behind.

"Who are you?" Sheetal asked.

"Just their business associate."

"Poor fellow, how would you know the wheelings and dealings of the celebrity world?" Anita Bhandari bemoaned theatrically.

"Death of a big shot such as MJ's grandson *is* a big event," explained Sheetal. "Social media engagement, flowers arrangement, photographers, make-up artist who specialise in the no make-up look, food ..." she continued. "Of course, she hasn't discussed charges formally, but big people always remember favours, and she will be rewarded handsomely in times of need."

"What a fantastic strategy," Shreyas agreed.

"It's called killing with kindness," Sheetal elaborated.

Shreyas floated towards another coterie, but was intercepted by Hasan.

"Where's MJ, the man himself?" he asked.

"He is resting after the heart attack," Urvashi explained. "They have converted a room here at Zanara into a hospital with 24-hour care."

"There is a queue of people waiting to see him, but only a select few are being granted permission," Shreyas said, pointing to the line.

"Let's go meet him," Hasan replied.

Their permission to meet MJ was granted, and they were ushered into a large room. MJ was lying on a king-sized bed with a lady tending to him, who Shreyas realised was Bhanu. An important-looking doctor was instructing his small team when he spotted Hasan.

"Is that you, Officer Hasan? I am Dr Gandhi; do you remember me? From the Mrs Punjabi murder case."

"Oh yes! Dr Gandhi, how are you?" Hasan replied with an insincere smile.

"I am fine. I had no idea you were working on this case! I have been the Jains' family doctor for many years. Surya couldn't have killed himself, you see. He wasn't the type. Do you know who the murderer is?"

"Aren't you a genius? A doctor and a detective all rolled into one! I didn't even know it was a murder!" Hasan exclaimed sarcastically. "Now that you have given us this tip, I think we should start by interrogating you!"

The doctor's face turned pale.

"He is only joking, doctor," Shreyas interjected quickly. The problem with Hasan was that he was capricious, unpredictable, and a verbal savage. Shreyas found it both exciting and excruciating to work with him.

"I am leaving now, Bhanu beta," the doctor said quickly. "I have instructed the nurses to stop these two medicines once his potassium levels look good." Glancing at Hasan, he continued, "And send the police away if you feel it is too draining for him."

"Yes doctor," Bhanu replied quietly.

"Sorry to disturb you at a time like this, but we need only a couple of minutes," Hasan spoke softly to MJ.

"Go on, you must do your duty," MJ said reassuringly.

Shreyas was surprised by the fortitude still burnishing from MJ's ailing body.

"I will get to the point – is there anyone who benefits financially from Surya's death?" Hasan asked as he advanced towards the bed.

"No, he didn't have any assets in his name. After me, my son Ashok will inherit everything."

"And your daughter?"

"In our custom, it is always the son. My will only has Ashok's name."

"Any other enemies; anyone else who would have a motive?"

"We are a well-known family and have our share of enemies, but no one who would want to kill Surya."

"You think it was an accident?"

"Yes. We just want the body to perform the last rites so that his soul can rest in peace."

"It's amazing, isn't it, MJ sahib? The people who don't have any money are willing to sell everything to get justice for their loved ones, and those who have all the money and power in the world want to squash the investigations, " Hasan commented.

"There is nothing to squash."

"Then what's the hurry?"

"Babuji," Bhanu cut in tearfully, "Kabir has landed and is on his way. He will be here any minute."

MJ's eyes welled up. Shreyas could sense the grief in every organ of his frame.

"You take good care of your father," Hasan said to Bhanu with a genuine concern that surprised Shreyas.

"My father and my son are the only reason I continue to live," she replied.

A beep on her phone suddenly grabbed her attention. "Excuse me, I must go now."

"One last question," Hasan halted her in her tracks. "Where were you at 8 p.m. last night?"

Shreyas could feel a shadow fall upon MJ's enervated face.

"I was in my room," she answered calmly. "We had the puja in the morning. I was up since 4 a.m. I was tired and slept early that night. Now if you will excuse me," she pleaded. "I really must go."

"Where were the others in the house?" Hasan continued.

"Everyone was home, in their respective rooms. The servants also retired early, " she replied, clenching her phone a little tighter.

"What about…," Hasan continued.

"I think this is enough for today. Please give us some privacy as we console Kabir," MJ said with a quiver in his voice.

Hasan nodded reluctantly.

Bhanu found her feet and rushed towards the main door.

Their car appeared out of nowhere in the driveway. A Vilas special. He could dissolve the parts of his vehicle and his body into thin air and then somehow assemble them and appear at precisely the right moment.

"If you continue this way, you are going to have a repeat of your earlier case," Urvashi said, letting out a sarcastic laugh in the sanctity of their car.

"Oh, the nagging wife is back again," Hasan sniggered.

Nobody spoke till they reached the metro station. Knowing that Shreyas took the train, Urvashi asked him, "Are you coming?"

Shreyas didn't know why, but he lied. "I am going to my in-law's place. I will take the bus from the bus-stop a little ahead."

"By enabling him," she said, waving her finger at Hasan, "you are making a big mistake."

He cringed as she slammed the vehicle's door on her way out. Hasan was nothing like what Shreyas had imagined. His speech was crude, and his thoughts always danced at the tip of his tongue, ready to unleash their wrath. Hasan was not the ideal idol, but Shreyas still somehow couldn't stop revering him. In this world of deceit, Shreyas believed that Hasan dared to speak the truth.

Like every Bollywood crazy Indian, Shreyas too had closely followed Sreelatha, the actress' case. He was stunned when Hasan, the Investigating Officer on the case, had declared that her death was due to accidental drowning in the bathtub. *Was he speaking the truth? Or, for the right price, was Hasan also willing to part with his morality?*

Chapter 15
Hasan

A fan whirs in the background, filling the room with white noise. The court is in session. The judge walks in. Everyone rises. A lawyer marches threateningly towards the defendant.

Lawyer: Officer, were you in charge of the case relating to the death of Sreelatha?

Defendant: Yes, sir.

Lawyer: You made some very slanderous comments. We have your statement on record. You said, 'she deserved what she got.'

Defendant: Sir, that was not a public statement. It was confined to the police department.

Lawyer: But does that make it acceptable, officer?

Defendant: Sir, everyone talks to their colleagues about cases. I am sure lawyers discuss cases in their chambers as well.

Lawyer: Facts! We only discuss facts. Anyway, what did you mean by that statement?

Defendant: She slept with a married husband. But once he divorced his first wife and married her, he turned tail and courted other younger women, prompting her to face the same fate as her husband's first wife. That is what I meant by she got what she deserved.

Lawyer: Isn't it true that you said the old hag was trying her best to retain her husband with all that plastic surgery?

Defendant: They were part of the same conversation.

Lawyer: Here is something different.

The lawyer presents some pictures to the judge.

Lawyer: Your Honour, Senior Inspector Hasan, as you can see from these pictures, was very friendly with the deceased's husband. He even attended many of their private events.

Hasan: Is that wrong?

Lawyer: No, it is not wrong. But, Your Honour, he made many reckless comments about the deceased at the time of her death, enough to cast a shadow of doubt that the investigation was prejudiced. It is a known fact that his wife eloping with his best friend has turned him into a misogynist who just cannot be trusted.

Hasan: My wife didn't elope; I would have respected her had she done that. She cheated, and she stayed. She waited to find out who got the promotion. Who would benefit her more!

Lawyer: That's not true. She was going to leave you. She just didn't have the courage to do it. That's because you are an awful person, officer! You are an evil, woman-hating monster!

Hasan: How dare you call me that!

A chair smashes to the ground.

Dr Poonawala caught the faint stirrings of a smile on Hasan's face. "This is not the story you shared previously," he said quietly.

"I know, but this is the dream that I had last night," Hasan smiled obscenely.

"You think this is all a joke," Dr Poonawala said, with his lips tightly pursed together. "We sit here, and you tell me your dreams, expecting a miracle. Who do you think I am? Some clairvoyant who will look into a crystal ball and interpret your dreams for you?"

"Isn't that something you do?"

"You have always taken these sessions lightly. I know you attend because you are not paying from your pocket, and you are not..."

"No, no doctor, you have gotten it all wrong," Hasan cut

him off. "I am not so selfish, I find them equally useless even when the department is paying for them."

Dr Poonawala was quiet. "There's no point in us continuing these sessions if you're going to be so abrasive."

"You are taking this way too personally. It's just that this whole process of therapy is warped. Talking just makes it worse."

"Let's finish for today then."

"Oh, I forgot to tell you the most important thing! I wet my pants! Now, why do you think that happened?" he asked innocently.

"This is not a joke. I want you to understand that. We'll continue once you intend to get better."

"You are losing your usual calm temperament, doctor. Worse, you think I am making this up," Hasan said, jumping out of his seat. "Maybe you're the one needing a therapist..." he added before walking out.

On the street, Hasan was feeling quite smug about riling up his garden-variety therapist when his phone rang. He knew it was his father. He felt bad for him. Abu was the only person who believed in these therapy sessions and never forgot to check on him post a session.

"Hello, Abu."

"Hello beta, are you busy? Am I disturbing you?" he inquired in his signature deferential tone that always pierced Hasan's conscience.

My son is a Crime Branch Officer; he would tell everyone with immense pride.

"Did you go for your session?"

"Yes, you know I did."

"I know you always go, even though you don't like it. It's just that I am old and senile, so I sometimes mix up the days, that is why I was checking."

Hasan hated the *'I am so old, hand me the Get-out-of-jail card please'*.

Abu continued. "I went to Mir Aloul Ashraf's Dargah, and the fakir gave me a *taweez* for you. Your mother would have wanted this."

The mention of his mother vexed him. Abu always threw in his Ammi whenever he wanted to coerce Hasan to do something. As a police officer, Hasan had often resorted to the same tactic; when he threatened to harm the family, even the hardened criminals would cooperate. But Abu's torture went a notch higher. He messed with Hasan's childhood memories.

"Abu, you know I don't believe in this stuff! Why do you do these things?"

"I am your father; I am only concerned for you. In my old age, I want to see my son become okay. Is that wrong?"

"I am fine and quite happy with myself," Hasan protested agitatedly. "You are the one who has a problem with me. Maybe you should wear the taweez!"

Chapter 16
Aadi

In the skies
17th June 2016

"Can I get you an extra duvet?"

Aadi reassured the air hostess that he was fine. As soon as he stood up to straighten his legs, he heard a voice call out his name. An attractive young woman was waving frantically at him.

"Gosh, how long has it been? How are you?" the woman said in her cheerful voice.

His brain frantically tried to place her, but came up with nothing.

"It's surely been long," he replied, nonchalantly.

"How's Megh doing?"

"Wait, you know Megh?" he blurted out.

"Aadi, what is wrong with you? She stole you from me!" she cackled.

Suddenly, the images of a night flashed before his eyes, and he remembered: The woman was Rhea; he had slept with her.

"Madam, sir, may we request you to lower your voices. It is disturbing the other passengers," the air hostess interrupted them.

"Of course, of course. We will chat later," Aadi said to her and settled down in his seat. Rhea had stirred the dregs of his memory.

Three years ago
Aadi's taxi entered the sliding entrance gates of Emporis Apartments

– the Wadhwa clan's Ayodhya; a twenty-five-storeyed, state-of-the-art residential building on the coveted Pali Hill.

Aadi's father, Vasudev Wadhwa, had thought he had bought a piece of nature when he had purchased a timid bungalow nestled on top of a hill lined by trees on both the steep and the mellow sides of the hill. Little did he know that this vegetation would be tamed to pave the way for Mumbai's very own Beverly Hills.

Some years later, Vasudev sold his bungalow, which was culled to the ground, and from its ashes arose the Emporis. Aadi's mother, Sheela, had been delighted with the rising tower. An elite socialite and the President of the Lioness Club, the address on her name card was her most dazzling ornament, and it carried enough clout to guarantee a full house for all her parties. She would have been upset to know that her death ceremony at the same address was not labelled 'houseful'.

After Sheela's death, Aadi moved to the US, and an inconsolable Vasudev took recourse in religion. The house became a waiting room, where the family abruptly met between flights. Only Aadi's sister, Avanti, an upcoming supermodel taking the Indian fashion fraternity by storm, would frequent the Emporis; it was here she soared high on all her notorious cannabis-fuelled parties.

Every August, Aadi visited India. His homecoming had never indented anyone's plan. Neither was Aadi expecting a reception party, but a party was waiting for him that day.

He rang the doorbell a couple of times before realising that the ear-splitting music coming from inside was neutralising the doorbell's ring. He was about to leave for a hotel when Ramu, their oldest house help, flung the door open.

"What's going on? Why didn't you send the driver to pick me up?"

"So sorry, Aadi baba, Avanti baby is having a party. Baby's friends took Munna to buy liquor. And Munna came back an hour ago, drunk."

Aadi was exasperated. He had been on Indian soil for less than three hours, but Mumbai's madness had already slunk into his life. All he had wanted was to be in his bed. He was manoeuvring the stairs to his room when Avanti ran up to him.

"Bhaiyyaaa! So good to see you," she said. "Let me introduce you to my friends." She held onto his arms, tearing him away from the handrail.

"Avanti please, my head is splitting. If you drag me down there, I will wrap up your party and send some of your friends home and some to the police station, as I can smell some stuff in here."

Avanti quickly freed her grip on him and ran down the stairs.

Around three in the morning, Aadi was awakened from his slumber. The jet lag had roused his latent hunger. Venturing into the kitchen, he saw the party still raging on. Polishing off his turkey sandwich, he was returning when the music changed to a desi number. A girl, atop his father's cherished mahogany table, was performing the infamous yet sultry 'Nagin' dance.

This nonpartisan music wave was new to India. When he had left India, it was considered sacrilege to play Hindi music at such sophisticated parties. India's independence had done nothing to erase its cultural submission to the West. But now Bollywood was legit; the youth dancing to the remixed version of the Nagin song was ample proof of its growing popularity.

Tickled by the scenery, a scotch on the rocks in his hands, Aadi decided to stay. The dancing stopped soon, and a heated discussion took place. The Nagin was in the centre of the huddle. She was the final authority on a wager on women's sexual pleasure. Educating her audience on the history of the G-spot, she claimed that it was Vatsyayana of Kamasutra fame and not Dr Graefenberg, who first referred to it in 300 CE.

To Aadi, she looked ordinary in an attractive way. Her eyes were hidden behind stern-looking glasses, but that didn't stop them from doing all the talking. The sparkle in her eyes had somehow lit up every corner of the dim-lit room. Succumbing to humidity, some wisps of her long hair had transformed into opinionated curls that hung around her face, making it look less oval and more round, like a moon. And in the centre of that moon was a nose bridge that was straight for the most part and then suddenly turned upwards, as if the tip was custom-made to stop the spectacles from slipping away. She was blowing smoke in a guy's face, who had pulled her to the dance floor once again and was revolving around her.

Avanti interrupted his watch. She wanted to introduce her friend Rhea, who began boring Aadi with her summer shopping plans.

"I finished my fashion degree from UK, and now I have my own boutique. I am off to London soon to shop for the new collection. What are your plans for the summer?" she asked.

"London is nice. I have no travel plans."

"How can you stay in Mumbai in the rains? It is so humid!"

"I like Mumbai in the rains, but London is also a beautiful city."

"Many new restaurants since I las— Oh fuck!" she yelped.

"What happened?"

"It's raining. Let's go in."

"It's just a drizzle."

"Let's go in, please," pleaded Rhea. "My blow dry will be ruined. And my shoes and my bag cannot have water on them. Fuck! Can I have a towel?"

They headed back to his room, where he offered her his towel, his bathroom, and his bed for some reason.

Rhea was fast asleep in his bed, having crashed after their sudden coitus, when Aadi tiptoed down once again. It was nearly dawn, and most of the party animals had passed out for the night. He noticed a girl tiptoeing. It was Nagin.

"Can you drop me home?"

"Excuse me? How had you planned to go back had you not discovered me?"

She flashed her phone light on one of the revelers asleep on the floor. "Well, he was supposed to be my ride. But he's passed out. Anyway, thanks, Daddy," the Daddy rolling off her tongue effortlessly.

"Wait; let me get my car keys."

"Where do you stay?" Aadi asked, once they were in the car.

"Just drop me at the closest railway station; I'll take the train to Churchgate. They should be starting soon."

"It's time for Daddy's morning tea anyway. I will drop you," he smiled, aware of the power of that smile.

"By the way, I am Aadi, Avanti's brother."

"Who's Avanti?"

They had barely covered a couple of kilometres when he jammed the brakes, "Avanti was your host for the night. I gather you gate-crashed the party, and I am dropping a gate-crasher home."

She laughed. Aadi could smell the cannabis on her.

"Sorry, I didn't mean to laugh, but are you always this uptight? Anyway, let me clear my name of this absurd accusation. My name is Megh, and I know your sister as Dipsy, or at least that's what her boyfriend, Harsh – my friend too – calls her. He lost a bet and was supposed to take the whole gang to this new nightclub, but the scrooge decided to shift the party to his — your sister's house."

"And why is my sister hanging out with such a loser?"

"That dick is great in bed," the words tumbled out of her mouth, "at least that's what Titsy – I mean Dips– ugh! Avanti says!"

Aadi laughed.

"Tea?"

"I have to get home soon. I have a job interview in a few hours, but a quick cutting chai won't hurt."

"Interview on a Sunday?" he asked, pulling up near a chaiwala.

"Yeah, apparently easier for working people to interview on a Sunday. It's with SGI. I am a Product Technologist. I have this outrageous idea for a chocolate, which I know will succeed."

"Sounds like a big disruption in the chocolate industry. Where are you working now?"

"BTC."

"The tobacco company?"

She nodded.

"They most likely won't be able to match BTC's package."

"I know. The package they pay me is for the industry, not for the job or the performance."

 "So why did you take up that job?"

"I had a loan to pay off."

"It's not easy to take a pay cut."

"I know. Even though I smoke, I don't want to sell tobacco. And if I ever need the money, I'll just marry a rich guy," she joked.

Aadi was smitten.

"It was nice meeting you, Megh. Good luck with your interview," he said, stopping the car near her colony's gate.

"Thanks."

He watched her walk away when acting on a sudden impulse, he called loudly. "Megh!"

She turned around, startled.

"Can I use your washroom? It's a long drive back."

Megh hesitated.

"I can wait till you freshen up and drop you off at SGI's office complex. I will google their location," he added quickly.

They rode up in the old Otis metal cage lift. The metal car wobbled till it aligned itself to the landing before halting resonantly, much like a tabalchi feverishly stroking the drums before striking the final beat of his taal.

 As she turned the key she said, "Keep your voice down! I don't want PM to wake up."

"Who is PM?"

"My aunt."

"What about AM? Sorry, bad joke, I mean your parents? You don't live with them?"

"Her name is Priya Madan, and my parents are dead."

"I am sorry to hear that. But it's 8.30 in the morning, won't she be awake?"

"No, she likes to get up late, and that works for me. I don't want to change that."

As they entered the house, she pointed to the door on the left. "That's the bathroom. I am going to my room to get ready."

Stepping into the bathroom, Aadi immediately bumped into a plastic bucket. Next to it, was a commode, sitting politely with its lid down, and serving as a table to a plastic bowl containing black dye. He placed the bowl in the sink, at the foot of a blurry mirror, festooned by a Hamam soap, Yardley talcum powder, and a wiry toothbrush, and had zipped his trousers halfway when the door flung open.

"Who are you?" said a woman in a nightie.

"Hello Auntieji, my name is Aadi. I came to drop Megh home."

"At this time? It's morning! I don't know what this girl does!" she said with a frown. "Anyway, thank you, son, for dropping her home. Can I offer you water?"

"Actually, I am extremely jet-lagged; I could use some tea."

"Of course, why not," she replied, surprised.

"You finish your job; I will keep it out for you. You want something to eat?"

"Yes, something to eat would be great. I am starving."

Aadi had finished gorging on two parathas and was devouring a papad when Megh reappeared wearing a white silk shirt with a navy-blue pencil skirt and said, "Let's go!"

Back in the car, offering to drive Megh didn't seem like a great idea to Aadi's jet-lagged and sleep-deprived mind. A couple of minutes later, he heard a soft snore. He looked at Megh, but she was busy reading something. He realised it wasn't her, it was him. He had dozed off for a split of a second. Luckily, she hadn't noticed. He drove on quietly. He didn't realize when he drifted off to sleep again, until he heard her scream, "Watch out!"

There was a loud crashing sound, and then everything went blank.

Chapter 17
The Sardar Police Station

Mumbai, 18th June 2016

The Surya Jain death case had been registered at the Sardar Police Station. The station, built in neo-classical architectural style with a hundred-year-old history, was one of the few buildings of Mumbai that mirrored the *shibboleth du jour* of an era gone by. The ground floor, with one of the oldest lock-ups in the city, had welcomed freedom fighters and underworld goons with equanimity. It had heard the sounds of aazan from the nearby mosque and the resounding bells from the Jain temple, but never had the two clashed. It had watched Bombay become Mumbai, the migrants become residents, and the residents become natives. The building was not bothered by the fuss being raked up for its centennial birthday. The renovations and refurbishments did not feel appropriate. There was no need for a big library or a conference room; it didn't suit an old edifice. But the station stood quiet, watching stoically, letting things happen. The nearby trading community had raised funds for a celebration and had gifted each officer with a lotus-shaped paperweight with 'Thank you for keeping us safe' etched in the centre of the base.

Fiddling with the paperweight, Hasan watched the conversation between Urvashi and her two young stooges unfold.

"Ma'am, our entire station is so proud that you are handling this high-profile case," Constable Aarti fawned.

"But you need to be careful," Constable Indra cautioned, "we all know that women usually don't make it to the senior-most positions within the force."

"Yeah, female officers must stand up and support each other. We are a minority here," Urvashi agreed. "We cannot waste our time like our male counterparts in the name of an investigation," she shot off a withered look in Hasan's direction.

"What do you think about this case, ma'am?" Aarti was curious.

"Looks like a straightforward open-and-shut case of accident to me."

"Then why a prolonged investigation?"

"Other departments interfere," Urvashi noted, shrugging her shoulders, "and we get blamed for it."

Hasan watched as the SGI employees lined up, waiting to be summoned, and decided to interrupt their soiree.

"*Devi Maate*!" Hasan exclaimed, folding his hands in a faux gesture of reverence. "If you are done with your discourse, let's start. Our witnesses have arrived."

The devotees broke up and scattered in different directions.

The interrogation room was a state-of-the-art 8x20 space with CCTV cameras, a glass wall separation, four chairs, and a table.

Shreyas escorted Praveen Lal in for the interrogation. As Praveen took a seat opposite Urvashi, Shreyas realised that Hasan had moved two chairs to the back of the room and was seated on one of them. He texted Shreyas, inviting him to sit next to him. Shreyas walked up to him and said, "Sir, Urvashi ma'am may not like it."

"May not like what?"

"She might not see the generosity of your heart that you are letting her lead the interrogation alone in the front. She might think that you see it as beneath you to talk to low-level employees," Shreyas explained hesitantly.

"Quite the contrary. She very much enjoys leading the interrogation. Some people feel very important because they get to ask questions. It doesn't matter to them whether the questions are important or not; just hearing their own voice make them happy."

Just then, he heard Urvashi shoot her first question, "Praveen, I understand you were on leave and have just resumed today."

Shreyas smiled sheepishly at Hasan.

"Yes, ma'am; I just flew in this morning."

"You were an assistant to Surya on one of the ongoing projects?"

"Yes, ma'am."

"What can you tell me about his character; what kind of a boss was he?"

"He was very moody. That was still okay, but he was also rude to his father."

"And *that* bothered you?" Hasan asked from the back of the room.

"Yes, sir, one must not be rude to their parents."

"Thank you so much; you can leave," Hasan said, undercutting Urvashi.

Praveen got up and rushed to the door, surprised that he was done so quickly.

Hasan caught Urvashi glaring at him.

"That guy had nothing important to say. You should dismiss these kinds of people early, or else we will only be listening to stories, like my therapist listens to me."

"Don't cut me ever again!" she rebuked.

His head down, with traces of a smile in its nascency, he folded his hands, seeking an apology as Carol, the next witness, walked in.

"How long have you been a part of the company?" Urvashi asked

"Only a few months, I am the new product technologist."

"What did you think of your boss?"

"I didn't really know him. He told me to work on a few ideas, that's all."

"And?"

"I was working on them."

"Was he happy with the progress?"

"Not really. Whatever I did was not good enough."

"How?"

"Exactly!" she said, thumping her fist on the table. "He couldn't explain. He just kept asking me to come up with something different like what our competitors are currently doing. I looked at our competition, and let me tell you – what they are doing is rubbish! Why would I make something like that? Just because that girl works there now?"

"Which girl?" Hasan interjected.

"Megh, the product technologist they fired. She now works for CFC. From the number of times Surya mentioned her name to me in our limited interactions, it seemed like he was obsessed with her. CFC is SGI's biggest competitor, but I personally think the obsession went beyond that. Anyway, I hardly know anything else. Can I leave now?" she asked.

"Yes."

"I have cross-checked all their alibis. Nothing unusual. I think we are done here," Urvashi said, pushing her chair back.

"It's interesting how even after two years, this girl Megh and the D'sire scandal keep coming up in our investigation. Carol has never met this Megh, yet she mentioned Surya was obsessed with her," Hasan said, sticking the pencil inside his eardrum.

"That means nothing," argued Urvashi. "He was obsessed with her and not the other way around. This investigation is going nowhere. There were no signs of a scuffle on the terrace, and no conclusive finger or footprints have been found. It was an accidental death!"

"D'sire had become a hoot," Hasan spoke distractedly. "I remember eating it and it *was* delicious. Then why is there nothing on the internet about it? There is something I want to show you guys," he said, firing up his laptop.

Both Shreyas and Urvashi peered over his shoulder.

His screen was full of images of Surya, but Hasan clicked on one in which he was holding a trophy. Hasan zoomed in, and suddenly the inscription at the bottom of the trophy became clear 'for the unprecedented success of D'sire'.

Then he zoomed in on another one: Standing on Surya's left was a pretty girl in a saree, her arm casually flung over his shoulders. Surya's one hand was around her waist, and he was smiling unabashedly at her. The photographer had managed to capture the moment in such a way that the sparkle in his eyes seemed to be spilling out of the laptop and filling the room.

There was a dark-skinned, clean-shaven man on Surya's right, but he was not smiling.

"This was the trio Mishal was talking about: Megh, D'sire's product technologist; Ali, the manufacturing manager; and Surya, the man himself."

Hasan digitally drew a question mark on the girl's forehead and continued, "Megh now works at CFC and lives in that very fancy building, Emporis. We must go and check the interior decoration of Megh's house," he said, grinning widely. "Also," he said to Shreyas, "track this Ali fellow down. Nobody knows where he is."

"Yes, sir," Shreyas replied enthusiastically.

"Did you not hear anything I said?" Urvashi said, her voice a loud shrill. "This whole D'sire case happened years ago. Tracking some ex-employees is a waste of the department's valuable time!"

"It's a lead that we must develop. Come on, it's not like you and me have better things to do," he said, chuckling.

Chapter 18
Urvashi

Mumbai, 18th June 2016

Hasan's casual jeer made Urvashi's stomach churn. She ran onto the road for some fresh air. She wanted to put him in his place. Unsure about what to do, she called the only person who castigated her often, but in strategy and second-level thinking, was second to none.

"How's it going?" Baba inquired.

"I want to kill Hasan! I am working with a misogynist."

"So, what they say about him is true?" Baba said excitedly. "I had heard conflicting reports."

"Like what?" she asked, frowning.

"That he is not a misogynist, a sharp-shooter with no filter, but not a woman hater."

"Oh, he absolutely is! He undermines everything I say."

"Is that because your arguments are baseless or is he really prejudiced?" Baba asked, always precise in his questioning.

Urvashi tried to think of a comment that would support her argument, but nothing came to her mind.

"The Surya Jain death case is an open-and-shut case, but Hasan wants to dig open an old story of that chocolate scandal that happened two years ago."

"Maybe there is some merit?"

"No chance. He is wasting my time, and because of that fool, I might come off looking incompetent. What should I do?"

"Don't worry. If he is running around in circles, let him. You play along for now. Let him take the lead and make a fool of himself. That would be good for you. Your time will come."

Chapter 19
Megh

Emporis Apartments
Mumbai, 20th June 2016

Megh queued up for elevator number four. Standing ahead of her were people who had returned after enduring a ten-hour day of corporate drudgery, endless rush-hour traffic, and senseless networking, only to sleep in withered beds in their microscopic apartments, happily mistaking them for their homes. She too, saw herself as one of them, except there was a gulf of difference between them and her. Her dwelling was a penthouse with a private elevator where she lived with her billionaire husband, Aadi Wadhwa; in a six-bedroom flat that was touted to be the most expensive condo on Pali Hill.

Today, she had to use the common elevator as the private one with access to her floor was undergoing maintenance. Allergic to elevator chitchat, Megh decided to busy herself with her phone. She was surprised to see a missed call from the elusive Rambo. She called him immediately.

"Hello, Megh. I read your proposal. We can't do it," Rambo said, getting right to the point.

"Why not?"

"It will cost the company too much."

"Not really. The chocolate will be one of a kind in India, I assure you," empty assurances fumbled out of her mouth as she sensed the project slipping away from her fingers. "It will be perfect for CFC's Corporate Social Responsibility as well," she added.

There was a pause. "Sethji won't approve," he said finally, in a quiet voice.

"I understand that traditionally business was done differently, but things are changing."

"Let me think about it again," he said finally. "By the way, Aadi had called me, he was looking for you."

Megh was taken aback. It was not like Rambo to engage in any kind of small talk. "Oh, he heard about Surya and wanted to check in on me."

"Okay. Was he a friend? Please accept my condolences."

"Thank you," she said, surprised at the sudden display of concern. "I will talk to you in the office tomorrow."

Aadi really shouldn't have called Rambo, she thought as she hung up. *Rambo wasn't that sharp, but Eliza and Sethji had probably picked up on something.*

"Megh darling, how are you doing?" someone called out her name. It was Pammi aunty from the seventeenth floor. The social media tattler of Emporis.

"I am fine; busy with work," she responded with a half-smile.

"You people are always busy. I sent you a WhatsApp for my *katha* tomorrow. Why have you not replied?" she pouted.

"Oh, I must have missed it."

"Come tomorrow. Not like last year, you didn't show up for any of my kathas."

"I will try."

"*Accha*, now give me some gossip," she persisted. "This Surya fellow who died, didn't you work for him a few years ago?"

Megh felt all eyeballs in the queue turn in her direction.

"In the same company, yes."

"Who killed him?"

"Killed him? No one knows that for sure."

"These influential people have many enemies; someone must have killed him."

The elevator hummed, announcing its arrival.

"I must go," Megh said.

"Of course, you must rush and get ready for your run!"

Megh was shocked that Pammi aunty knew about her daily exercise routine.

"Wait, I almost forgot to tell you," Pammi aunty added slyly, "the police are waiting in your house!"

Megh's heart started beating furiously.

The ride in the elevator felt longer than usual.

Finally, in the privacy of the stairwell of her floor, she took two quick drags from her vape before buzzing herself into her apartment.

"Didi, the police are here for you," Jazz, her help, announced.

"Is sir home yet?"

"No, not yet."

She found a party of three – two men and a lady officer, waiting for her in her living room.

"Hello Mrs Wadhwa, I am Officer Hasan, and this is Senior Inspector Urvashi and Sub-Inspector Shreyas."

"How can I help you?" Megh replied, holding her gaze straight at him.

"We wanted to talk to you about Surya Jain's death. I believe you both had a history together. I mean, you worked with him, and you guys created history together with D'sire. Such a desirable name! Didn't it win some popular choice or best innovation award in the confectionary market?"

"Yes."

"But there is no mention of it on the internet!" he remarked, shaking his head in obvious surprise.

"Someone must have taken it down. The whole ADR fiasco involving a vegetarian company was very controversial. Obviously, the company is not very proud of that outcome."

"But you were proud of it?"

"Yes, D'sire was my baby. My team and I worked hard on it."

"What happened when they found the animal rennet?" Hasan probed.

"I was fired."

"That must have hurt," Hasan interjected.

"It did. But shit happens."

"If that Toni Mehta was behind it, why were you fired?" Hasan asked.

"They didn't know it then, and I was the perfect scapegoat."

"And why were you the perfect scapegoat?"

Megh shrugged her shoulders. "I don't know. A woman trying to chart her own path in a man's world, I guess."

"Oh, you are another one of those quasi-feminists," he yawned.

"What do you mean?" Megh glared at him.

"Nothing, I admire women who want equal rights and are willing to fight for it. It's just that some women, like you, want equal rights and opportunities, but it doesn't bother you at all that you live in a penthouse owned by your husband. You would never be able to sustain this lavish lifestyle on your CFC salary. Anyway, let's not digress. You and Surya were very close. You didn't expect him to fire you."

Megh's ears went red. "Surya and I were workmates, that's it. He had nothing to do with firing me. If anything, he was against it. It was the decision of the board."

"Ali was also a part of this triumvirate. Are you in touch with him?"

"No, I cut contact off with everyone from SGI after I was fired."

"What about Surya? When did you last meet him?"

"On the day I was fired. That was about two years ago."

"And you haven't seen him or spoken to him since?"

"No."

"And what were you doing the night he died?"

"My daily routine – I came back from work, went for a run around the apartment block, and then came home and slept."

"You do that every day?" Hasan enquired.

"That's what *daily* means, officer."

"Whom did you meet that day between 8-11 p.m.?"

"My husband was out of town, but I obviously met Jazz, my help, and the people who saw me running."

"That's the problem. Jazz and your building's security guard saw you leave and come back, but nobody really saw you running," Hasan said.

"I don't know how to prove that," Megh said, shrugging her shoulders.

"Do you remember meeting anyone?" Hasan asked.

"Not really! When I am running, I don't stop and talk to anyone."

"Do you think Surya could have killed himself?"

"No, I don't think so…, at least not the Surya I knew. He was too much in love with himself to do that."

There was the click of a key, and the main door opened. Aadi walked in. He hid the surprise of seeing cops in his house well.

"Aadi," he introduced himself. "What's this about, officer?" he asked, sitting on the armrest of Megh's chair. He put his hand on Megh's thigh.

"Routine investigation," Hasan said. "Your wife was just telling us what she thinks happened to Surya."

"I think he got high as usual and probably slipped to his death."

"And do you?" Hasan asked Megh.

"Do I what?"

"Get high?" Hasan asked.

"I used to," Megh admitted, "when I was at SGI. But I quit."

"Did he ever force you?"

"No, never."

Aadi butted in. "She is clean now. We are trying to conceive."

"Are we done, officer? It's been a long day, and I am getting late for my run."

"Yes, that will be all," Hasan said, as they headed for the door.

"Oh, I almost forgot. You insist that you and Surya were only workmates," he said, holding up a picture, "but this picture tells a different story."

She recognised the image from afar before scoffing. "Officer, the problem is that you will see a flaw in every picture. It is a part of your work, I guess. Let's cut a deal – you don't have to believe what I say, and I don't have to say what you want to believe. Find me one person at SGI who worked with us and thinks something was going on between Surya and myself," she said with finality.

A smile formed on Hasan's face as he stared at her for a long time before tossing the photo at her and heading out of the door.

Megh held the picture in her hand. She remembered the day and the moment perfectly. The picture was taken at D'sire's success party. Surya was high and had just confessed his love for her.

She felt Aadi's scent close to her body, reminding her of his presence. If he suspected something, he didn't show it. "I am going to change," she said and went to her room. With the door locked firmly, she pulled out her phone and deleted her call history.

Chapter 20
Shreyas

Mumbai, 20th June 2016

Outside the Emporis lobby, the Mumbai rains welcomed them with their first offerings of the monsoon season.

Vilas had once again spotted them through the downpour with utter ease. He had even tuned into the channel with the most love-struck radio jockey couple. This time, when the jeep stopped at the railway station, Urvashi got off without asking Shreyas if he wanted to commute together.

Suddenly Shreyas heard Hasan hum along to Kishore Kumar's *'Ek Ladki Bheegi Bhaagi Si'*.

"What do you think about this *ladki*, sir? Megh, is she *seedi - saadi*?" Shreyas asked, proud of the way he had inserted the song in his question.

"She is hardly seedi-saadi; more like spiky and spicy," Hasan laughed.

Shreyas looked at him, amused. The rains had put Hasan in a good mood.

"Because she was outspoken and honest?" Shreyas asked.

"Honest, no. Outspoken, for sure."

"Why not honest, sir?"

"She is the only one so far without an alibi. What about you? You liked her?"

"No," Shreyas said, shaking his head vigorously. "I feel bad for her husband. Nobody can control her," he said, as if she was a wild horse who needed to be reined in.

"What do you mean?"

"She is the blunt type. She won't even respect elders."

"Why should one respect elders if they are talking nonsense and disrespect someone younger if they are making sense?" Hasan argued. "Our traditions bully us. If people are worthy of respect, we should respect them regardless of their age or gender. The plight of women in this country is ironic. Why do they need to be controlled? We worship them in temples, but want to control them in our homes," Hasan wryly commented. "You, the good guys, believe in all this controlling crap and the world calls me a misogynist!"

Shreyas felt the phone in his pocket vibrate; he jumped as he recognised the number. It was the Police Commissioner.

"Hello sir!" he said, the respect oozing out of his every pore.

"Hello young chap, how are you doing?"

"I am fine, sir."

"Can you please give the phone to my man, Hasan? He has many virtues, but timely attention to a ringing phone is not one of them," the Commissioner sighed.

"Sir?" Shreyas tried to decode the garbled message.

It was the first time he had directly engaged with the commissioner's British English, and he was underwhelmed. *How could a person heading the police force take so much time to say something so simple? He preferred the use of brevity by his milkman's son, who said 'off hogaya' to relay his father's death.*

Hasan unenthusiastically took the call.

"Hasan, my boy, why are you not answering your phone?"

"Busy with the investigation, sir. I was going to update you soon," he lied.

"What is the progress on the case?"

"Going well, sir. We have a lead. A woman called Megh, who used to work for SGI, is the prime suspect as of now.

She had a spat with Surya, and she doesn't have any concrete alibi about her whereabouts on the night of his death."

"When did they have a falling out?"

"Two years ago."

"You sure it is still relevant?"

"Sir, it's eerily similar to Mira Deshmukh vs the State case. She took revenge after fifteen years! When this Megh was fired, it was quite a scandal. "

"When will they release the body?"

"I am waiting on the lab reports."

"Tell them to hurry up and keep me posted."

"Yes sir."

Descending from the jeep, Shreyas replayed his conversation with Hasan about Megh in his head as he made way to his chawl. The world called Hasan a misogynist, and yet, he had spoken like a feminist. *Could someone be both?*

"Dry yourself quickly and change your clothes. Dinner's almost ready," Savita said. The living room was fragrant with the smell of ghee as Savita walked in holding a gleaming *pooranpori* for him.

"How's the case coming along?"

"It's confusing. Urvashi ma'am feels that it's an accident. Hasan sir believes that there is more to the story. I am stuck in between. I used to believe that these rich people have so much money, they must not be having problems. But that is not the case at all; they also have so many problems. Money is the source of all evil."

"I don't think so. Money is just an object," Savita commented. "What you choose to do with that money is what causes trouble. I would like us to have more money, to get a fan in the kitchen, maybe."

"Too much ambition this one has," her mother-in-law quipped from in front of the TV.

"What's wrong with ambition?" Shreyas asked. "Whole day, you are telling Shivu to study hard, that he has to become a big man. He should have ambition, but a woman should not?"

Savita stopped midway and stared at him. *Had she heard him correctly? Was her husband making a point against his mother?* Savita sensed a schism in Shreyas' thinking; something felt different. She wanted to talk to him about opening her salon. Even though she lived in a small home, her dreams for her salon were big.

"This murder case is making you mad; you are seeing all these rich people and behaving pish-posh like them," his mother complained. "And you, bahu, don't talk about such things. It will only have *burra asar* on the child."

Savita's mother-in-law used burra asar as her Brahmastra, her ultimate weapon to squash any rebellion while making Savita believe that it was all for her child's benefit. *Burra asar, my foot!* Savita muttered to herself.

After clearing the plates, Savita went back to the living room and heard a soft snore. Her mother-in-law's eyes were closed, and Shivu was also preparing for bed. She snuggled up to Shreyas, who was watching a news debate on TV. She decided to take her chance.

"I have been meaning to talk to you," she whispered, playing with his hair.

"*Bol,*" he said softly, fondling her breasts.

"I want to work after delivery."

"We will see," he said.

"I want a salon of my own. You know that Sheena? she takes care of her baby *and* runs her own salon now."

Without warning, Aai awakened and her shrill voice boomed over the noise of the television. "All this is not allowed in our family. We have told you so many times before!"

Shreyas and Savita cut their conversation short. Savita tossed and turned for a while, trying to find a suitable position for her enormous belly. She sensed Shreyas lying awake.

"What's the matter?" she asked. "Is the case bothering you?"

"No, it's not the case. I am just thinking," he said. "The plight of women in this country is ironic. We worship them in temples, but want to control them in our homes." Shreyas recited from memory. "Hasan sir said this today. I think he was talking about my house."

Though Savita didn't fully grasp what Shreyas had said, she felt that her Shreyas was changing. *This Hasan sir seemed to be a very kind-hearted man.* She made a mental note to invite him over for a meal so she could personally thank him.

Chapter 21
Chana

Imperial Towers I
21st June 2016

"Hello Chana, the police are here to speak with you." It was the receptionist on the intercom.

Chana's heart skipped a beat. *Had the police found out about her past? Did they know about her illegal status in the country?*

"Do they want to speak specifically *to me* or anyone in the office?" she asked.

"I don't know," the receptionist was vague.

Chana was getting tired of this new bird-brained receptionist who had been hired recently after Surya's death to sit in the lobby and personally screen all SGI visitors.

"Then find out," Chana replied angrily.

The recorded on-hold commercial, heavy on a British accent, started rolling.

A million thoughts ran through Chana's mind before the receptionist came back on the line.

"The officer wants to know something about some D'sire's success party. He said you would know," she said.

So, the police wanted to talk to her about Surya, Chana sighed with relief. She had always wanted to be the go-to person in the company. The fact that people came up to her desk with their petty issues and wanted her to solve them gave her a sense of control in the office. Striving to be approachable, she would laugh at the jokes, no matter how silly, and would always make time for polite conversation. But something was changing within her. The exterior façade was the same, but on the inside, she didn't feel like smiling anymore, especially after Surya's death.

She saw officer Hasan taking long strides toward her desk.

"Hello, officer! You have come alone today?" she asked with a warm smile.

"Yes; the other officers are busy, so I thought I would come along and spend a couple of minutes in your wonderful company."

"How can I help you?"

Hasan carefully unfolded a copy of the D'sire success party photo and laid it out neatly on her desk.

"I want to know more about the day this picture was taken. It is like a keyhole through which we can see a world that once existed, but since has been destroyed. I want to know everything that leads up to this picture."

"I don't know what you are looking for, but I will tell you what I know." She led him to one of the break-out rooms, rolled down the blinds, and took a deep breath before narrating the story.

"It was a crazy year as D'sire had won all the awards in the Food Innovation category. For the first time, MJ announced an all-expense-paid party in Agra, on the stunning grounds of Hotel Amar Villas with the Taj Mahal in the backdrop. The theme for the party was 'The Moghuls.' The entire outdoor area had a traditional Indian feel with dholwalas and qawwali singers adding to the buzz."

"Move on, move on," Hasan muttered.

"We had assigned seating. Surya was at the main table with his parents and grandparents. Toni and Bhanu were at my table, along with Megh and Ali. Toni started kicking up a fuss. He was upset that he had been relegated to an employee table. He complained to Bhanu, and she quietly got him a seat on the main table.

Megh was getting a lot of attention, and that was annoying me. I told her that her silver locket didn't match her gold saree. But she told everyone about its sentimental value and that impressed everyone even more."

"Then?" Hasan egged her on.

"There were speeches. After Surya's speech, Mishal asked him something about the chocolate and how it melted so easily. Before Surya could respond, Megh took the mic and said, 'How it melts is a secret, and this secret is not to be revealed, but to be experienced!' She then unwrapped the chocolate and put it in her mouth. There was thunderous applause. The entire office was euphoric. The picture was taken around that time. After that, Ali Asger, the other guy in that picture, came rushing and told us that he had just received a call from Nigeria that his mom had suffered a heart attack. He immediately notified HR; Surya even offered to pay for his flight – which he declined – and left. After some time, I went to the ladies' room. It was in the main lobby, far from the hotel grounds, and Toni decided to follow me. He started hitting on me. I somehow wriggled my way back. Megh sensed something was wrong when I returned. I told her about what had happened, and she was livid. She advised me to file a complaint against Toni, but I refused."

"Why did you refuse?"

"What's a complaint against some butt squeezing that nobody witnessed going to do? If I quit, what would I tell my future employer? If you state sexual harassment as the reason, they think you are a troublemaker."

"Megh got mad at me," she continued. "All our virgin drinks had been laced with alcohol, and we had been smoking up. We ended up saying unspeakable and nasty things to each other. I dragged her down about her billionaire husband while she accused me of trying to seduce Surya. I guess that was the last straw, because I remember getting angry and slapping her."

"Were you trying to seduce Surya?"

"What nonsense!"

"Who witnessed your little cat fight?" Hasan asked.

"Surya."

"What did he say?"

"He was angry with me for slapping Megh!"

"Chana, would you say that Surya and Megh were having an affair?"

She was quiet for a while before she uttered, "No."

Chapter 22
The Tekchands

Mumbai, 22nd June 2016

Sethji quickly went to his den and shut the door. The place had been done up like an old Edwardian library, with easy brown armchairs and a large mahogany desk. The wall behind his desk bragged of a constellation of trophies and certificates won by the Tekchand family.

All of them had been doctored carefully by artists who claimed to do just that for a living.

Sethji had also wanted an honorary doctorate and had written to many universities requesting them to confer him with one for a small processing fee. Of course, none of the noteworthy ones had obliged. Taking matters into his own hands, he conferred the honorific title of Seth upon himself. Only the 'Women's Finals Champion for Tennis, Malta' trophy deserved to be on the wall. It belonged to his daughter, Reema.

Sethji perched himself gingerly on the single-seater and pulled out a newspaper cutting from the bottom drawer of the desk. The headlines, even after so many years, jolted him.

Two households, both alike in dignity, in fair Maldives, where we lay our scene...

Star-crossed lovers, Reema and Rajvir, end their lives by self-immolating, thus meeting the same fate as Romeo and Juliet. Reema, the effervescent twenty-two-year-old daughter of Seth Tulsidas Tekchand, hopelessly fell in love with the gentle Rajvir, nephew of the famed MJ of SGI. When their families disagreed, they secretly tied the knot at a registrar's office in the Maldives with two friends as witnesses.

Little did the couple know that the three-star hotel they were staying in had a strategic partnership with SGI. MJ quickly tracked down the couple's whereabouts. When the news leaked, the duo doused themselves in petrol and died without pomp and parade. Neither of them shouted for help, bearing their fate silently. The Jains convinced that the girl Reema had cast a spell on their well-mannered, cultured son, cremated their son in a private ceremony.

Sethji folded the paper quickly, unable to read any further. *How could they publish such utter nonsense about his Reema?*

Initially, when Sethji had learned about the affair, he wasn't jubilant. But the pedigree demanded a reconsideration. After all, the boy was a Jain. The more he thought, the more he was convinced that this could be the perfect match for Reema. His daughter would marry into one of India's wealthiest families.

Sethji had anticipated some resistance as the Jains were known to keep their children on a tight leash. Still, with time, he thought that they would be more accepting, maybe even grateful. After all, the Tekchands were of good social and economic standing, and Reema was an extremely beautiful girl. He and his wife had been amassing wealth and jewels from the day she was born and were willing to pay for a lavish wedding. A lot of proposals had come for Reema, but Sethji had his heart set on a big fish. It seemed like the fish had come to the shore looking for him.

But MJ did not relent, and matters got worse. He lost his Reema. What hurt him even more was that the Jains' narrative, off the record, always projected Reema as a slut lacking in values. Of course, the two families outwardly maintained a respectful relationship, but on the inside, Sethji couldn't wait to expose the real Jains to the world.

Slowly and steadily, he built his base in Mumbai. He was waiting to launch his best brand yet – Rambo – and make the right connections through his son's wedding. He was not looking for wealth. He was looking for someone who yielded influence – an influencer.

When he met Avanti's father, Vasudev Wadhwa – a writer, a businessman and a former international diplomat – he was completely consumed by his charisma. *What finesse and pedigree this man must have bred in his progeny*, he wondered. There was some chatter about the breakup of Vasudev's daughter, Avanti's engagement with Subu, the skipper of a league cricket team who had not made it to the Indian national squad. Media had splashed photos all over the newspapers. Sethji liked what he saw, especially her pictures in a compromising position with the cricketer. The next day, he called Vasudev and spoke to him about a possible alliance between his son Rammeher, and his daughter, but Vasudev politely declined stating that his daughter had just come out of an intense relationship and would be not interested in starting a new one.

Sethji was disappointed in him. He had credited him with more prescience. *This was the problem with these very educated people; they did not have enough hunger in them to make a killing.*

A couple of months later, he again contacted the Wadhwas – this time he aimed direct – he called Avanti and discussed the possible purchase of a certain cricket team. This particular team had not been performing well, and Sethji felt a change in ownership and management could make all the difference. He promised to retain Subu as the skipper of the team.

Of course, Avanti would have to become a member of the Tekchand family if she wanted to run the show. He was in no pressing hurry – she could meet with Rambo and then decide.

The spur in her voice told him that the deal had already been sealed. The meeting would be a mere formality. He advised Rambo to take Avanti on their private jet to Malta to visit their family's mansion that they still maintained. He knew the cavalcade of wealth would be too much to resist. He also understood Avanti's need to deride Subu. He had found the right bahu for the family.

Vasudev died a month before his daughter's engagement. Though extremely private, the engagement ceremony had been the town's talk for months. Soon after his engagement, Rambo became a brand in India. He had found his influencer.

And now Sethji wanted his revenge. He wanted to trample SGI.

Chapter 23
Zanara

Mumbai, 23rd June 2016

The Commissioner of Police had given his word to MJ that the police would complete their interrogation in the outhouse, away from the prying eyes of the public pouring in to offer their condolences at Zanara.

Constable Pandya Singh led them to the outhouse where a queen-sized bed had been expelled from its room to make space for a table and four chairs.

Tea and snacks arrived almost immediately.

A motley crew of servants and drivers waited outside in the living room for their turn to be interrogated.

"Wow, there are at least three servants per house member," Shreyas whistled with awe, "and there's enough religious representation too."

"What do you mean?" Hasan asked, munching on masala peanuts that had come along with the steaming dhoklas and tea.

"You mean her?" he said, pointing to a lady in a burqa seated alone on a fake leather couch.

"And him," Shreyas pointed to an elderly man at the other end of the room, wearing a dhoti and sipping tea.

"Let's call him in first."

As usual, Hasan pulled two chairs behind, letting Urvashi lead the interrogation.

"What's your name?" Urvashi asked the man.

"Pramukh, sahib."

"What do you do in the house?"

"I am *Maharaj*, sahib."

"What does that mean?" Hasan laughed. "You think you are some sort of royalty?"

"He means to say he is the cook. Brahmin cooks in traditional families are called 'maharaj' out of respect," Shreyas explained.

"What illusions of self- grandeur!" Hasan said, amused. "And why are you calling her 'sahib'?" he quizzed. "She is a woman, can't you see?"

"But I am answering to you, sahib," Maharaj replied, confused.

For the first time, it hit Shreyas the implicit bias that a woman faces every day. Urvashi was asking the questions, but Hasan was getting the answers.

"How many years have you worked in this house?" Urvashi continued.

"Twenty-three years in the same household. Surya was a baby when I came. I didn't kill him!" he cried.

"You stay here, in the house?"

"Yes, sahib."

"Sharing or alone?"

"Alone. All the servants sleep in the shared quarters on Minus 2, but I have a separate room."

"Minus 2?"

"Yes, Minus 1 in the basement is parking and cinema room, and Minus 2 is the servants' quarters."

"What were you doing on the night of Surya's death?"

"We had the tula daan ceremony in the morning. For dinner, I made simple *dahi ki kadi* and rice; everyone went to their rooms early."

"What did you do after that?"

"I was exhausted; I went to sleep."

"And the next morning?"

"I usually get up at four a.m., but that morning I overslept."

"Alcohol?"

"I am a brahmin; I don't drink."

"We would like to check your kitchen and your quarters."

"I cannot take you there, sahib."

"Why?" Hasan probed angrily.

"Sahib, you are a Muslim," he said hesitantly. "You eat *maas*; my religion and I will be finished if I bring a meat-eater to my room."

Religion was surely powerful, Shreyas observed. Suddenly the man who the maharaj was directing his responses to had been demoted because of his religion.

"Make sure you check his quarters after we are done here," Hasan said.

"Can I go now?"

"Yes," Hasan ordered, "and send that lady in the purdah."

The woman took a seat. Only her kohled eyes were visible through the veil.

"What is your name?" Urvashi began.

"Nasima."

"Nasima, how come you live here in such a staunch Hindu house?"

"Political reasons," she said, simply.

"What do you mean?"

"Many years ago, an NGO saved me from my abusive marriage. I needed a shelter, a good home, as I was both physically and mentally broken," she said, looking at them, her eyes unblinking. "The lady who ran the NGO was a very influential woman, and she was good friends with the Jains. She told them to let me in, but they refused as I was a Muslim. But she convinced them that it would look good for

Ashok *bhaisa's* eventual political career to provide shelter to a helpless Muslim lady."

"You are the only female staff in the house. Where do you sleep in Minus 2?"

"No, Bhanu didi will never allow such a thing. I sleep in her room."

"The cook is okay with you in the house?"

"He is not my boss. Even though he doesn't let me enter his kitchen, I am the one who does all his work."

"What do you mean?"

"I buy all the groceries for the house. Every evening, I go to the nearby market with Mukesh, the driver, and we buy everything from Bhanu didi's list."

"You did the shopping even on the day of Surya's death?"

"Yes, we didn't know then."

"What did you buy that day?"

"*Toori, dudhi, mooli,*" she started counting on her fingers.

"What are they?" Hasan asked.

"Vegetables, sir, what else? And kale leaves for Surya bhaiya."

"You have the bill of the items you bought that day?"

'Yes, didi remembers me giving her the bill for that day. Should I get it?"

"Yes, and send the driver in on your way out."

As the investigation continued, Shreyas learned about a different world that lived underneath, in Minus 2. A pan chewing man, the driver corroborated Nasima's story, but not before conveniently slipping in that she wasted too much time flirting with vegetable vendors. Next came the assistant cook, who was sure that the maharaj smoked chillum, even though nothing was found in his room during a search later. There were a couple of cleaners belonging to the Jamadaar community who worked for the Jains, but had not been allowed shelter because of their caste. The people of Minus 2 could come up, interact with this world, and return to their own again. They were free to work, visit, and even linger sometimes, but never truly belonged to the ground level of Zanara.

For the rest of the day, they interrogated the family members: Bhanu, MJ, Ashok, Sharda: they all had a synchronised narrative and watertight alibis – they all talked about the tula daan ceremony, its importance, the women and staff retiring early, and the men going to work. They all denied any discord between the three pillars of the three generations, dismissing what Roma had said as useless office gossip.

They were getting ready to leave when Sharda entered the room.

"I hope everything went okay."

"Yes it did, thank you so much," Shreyas replied.

Sharda looked around nervously before talking. "Actually, I wanted to speak with you, but I don't want you to share what I tell you with anyone."

"Of course," Hasan replied reassuringly as he whisked her to the empty room, securing the latch on the door as soon as Shreyas and Urvashi managed to slide in.

Her *ghunghat* resolute, Sharda lowered herself in the single-seater recliner, her fleshy arms adding another layer of cushioning to the armrest. "Since..." she paused to push a lump down her throat. "Since my Surya died, I have been looking for answers. Why should it happen to him? *To us.*"

"Then my friend took me to her tarot card reader," she continued, "and when I asked her the cause of death, she pulled out a card, and it showed – murder."

"Thank god, at least tarot card readers agree with my theory," Hasan said sarcastically.

"I am sure my Surya was murdered. For revenge," she continued.

"Revenge?" Hasan asked.

Suddenly she was a million miles away. "My father-in-law, Babuji, has a brother who lives in Gujarat. He had a son Rajvir. A polite and well-behaved boy, he was just five years older than my Surya. Babuji called his brother and told him that he wanted Rajvir to start the Maldives operations for SGI. He wanted an insider; someone he could trust completely. He almost pleaded for Rajvir to join him. Everyone thought this would be an excellent opportunity for Rajvir, as he was a little shy.

"But in Maldives, Rajvir fell in love with a girl who had come there for a holiday. Babuji was against the alliance. She was from a decent family, but if he let him go ahead, then we would be setting a precedence for the other youngsters in the family to marry just about anyone. They could bring Muslims and Catholics, and god knows who all to pollute our name."

Shreyas winced, but a naïve Sharda remained unaware of the inappropriateness of her comment.

"He went too far to break the alliance. Basically, he wanted to break Rajvir's resolve and make an example out of it. Rajvir couldn't handle it, and he committed suicide. Both the boy and the girl set themselves on fire... It was a terrible death. One thing that nobody knows is that Babuji had arranged for a special plane to fly Rajvir to London to get the best treatment for his burn wounds, but he died before the plane took off. The girl briefly survived. He could have saved her life by flying her to London for treatment. But he called it off, saying she was not his problem. By the time her family got to Maldives from Malta, she was dead. But we could have saved her. Babuji has a lot of connections in Maldives, so everything was hushed up, and no one knows this part of the story."

"Who was the girl?" Urvashi asked.

"She was the daughter of Seth Tulsidas Tekchand, owner of CFC," Sharda replied. "I feel that maybe Sethji has somehow found out about the plane. Sometime ago, he moved his base from Malta to Mumbai. We have our offices in Imperial Towers I and CFC took office space in Imperial Towers II. Even in business, CFC is head-to-head in competition with SGI. When we fired that girl, Megh, they took her in. They are always close at our heels. Too close," she said, emphasising on this connection.

"Sir, Rambo, Sethji's son, is getting married to Avanti, Aadi's sister. It is going to be a star-studded wedding," Shreyas added.

"Wow!" Hasan chortled. "This is turning out to be a story of three powerful families – the Jains, the Tekchands, and the Wadhwas interlinked in their crimes."

"Please don't say anything to anyone or I will get into deep trouble, but I do want you to investigate. I feel maybe somehow the Tekchands took their revenge. If my son was killed, then I want justice for him."

As they were leaving Zanara, Hasan's phone rang. It was the Commissioner of Police, but Hasan was eager to speak with him this time.

"Hello, sir."

"Hello, my boy!"

"You have called at the right time. We have a huge lead," Hasan said, cautiously excited.

"What is it?"

"Sir, we just finished our interrogations at Zanara, and Sharda Jain, MJ's daughter-in-law, has shared some juicy bits of information that could have a big impact on the case."

"Like what?"

"Sir, it was shared in confidence. Let me do a fact-check on the intel shared. But if it is true, then it will shake up Mumbai's high society."

"I am not buying into any of this till you don't give me a name," the commissioner cut him off.

Hasan hesitated and finally spoke in almost a whisper, "Seth Tulsidas Tekchand."

The commissioner inhaled sharply at the other end, "You are going after a very big fish, a shark really."

"I understand, sir."

"Hasan, are you sure there is some merit in your theory? I am beginning to wonder if you are trying to find a murderer for a crime where none exists," he said. "Do whatever you need to, but quick!"

Then he hung up.

Chapter 24
Sethji

Mumbai, 24th June 2016

Sethji picked up a report from his table. It was the Divine Cocoa Project.

Consumer trends are moving towards ethical buying. Organic, vegan, and fair trade are not just buzzwords that people use in conversations anymore; there is truly a shift in belief systems.

The Divine Cocoa project is the perfect combination of business and sustainability goals, providing CFC with an opportunity to achieve self-sufficiency while making a meaningful difference in the community. The farmers will benefit tremendously from the project, while CFC will be the first Indian company to manufacture fully fair-trade-compliant chocolate on a mass scale.

"I don't care about this rubbish project. I am not interested in helping farmers," Sethji said, flinging the file back on the table.

"What Megh is proposing with her fair-trade certification is a win-win for all parties," Rambo explained. "All big companies are going this way. These guidelines are designed to redeem the imbalance of power in trading relationships, the uncertainties of unstable markets, and the injustices of conventional trade. CFC will have the best chocolate in Divine, and we will be seen as a pioneer with this CSR move. It will only help our bottom line."

"She is not a business person, this Megh," Sethji grumbled. "I want Divine chocolate to taste better than D'sire. That's all. She is a product technologist and that's all she should worry about."

He further asserted, "All these certifications will add to our cost. We gave her this job because your brother-in-law Aadi insisted, and because I like him. That doesn't mean we have to listen to her ludicrous ideas."

As usual, Rambo began doubting his decision. Sethji's words had a way of doing that. "So, what do you suggest we do now?"

"I just got an idea," Sethji had an ungodly smile plastered across his face. "Where is Avanti nowadays? Why doesn't she ever come to the office?"

"She doesn't like coming to the office," Rambo said. He was secretly thankful for that.

"Our team Mumbai Musketeers is playing tomorrow at Wankhede Stadium," Sethji said. "Why don't you guys visit the players? You are the franchise owners, after all. Meet with them. Cricket is something Avanti enjoys as well. In fact…" he said smiling even more, "invite her for lunch to the office and then take her to the stadium. I will also invite Megh; she is Avanti's sister-in-law. Once you are married, I will get Avanti to say No to this Megh. Avanti will relish the opportunity to play boss to her sister-in-law! "

Rambo's palms started sweating profusely. He wondered if it had anything to do with spending the day with his drop-dead gorgeous fiancée.

Chapter 25
Megh

Mumbai, 25th June 2016

Megh had received an email from Sethji's PA, inviting her for a private lunch. Suspicious about the sudden act of benevolence, she had made a few calls and learned the real reason behind the invite. Avanti was coming to the office. Megh figured that between an anxious Rambo and an in-awe Sethji, they probably needed someone to have a normal conversation with Avanti. Avanti demanded an audience, and as her sister-in-law, Megh, was the chosen one.

The lunch was to be served in the conference room, which also doubled up as Sethji's office. Sethji didn't see any reason for maintaining a separate conference room, as there never was a meeting without him. With him, everything needed to have a utilitarian angle, or else it was pointless. He would even slice off his nipples – vestigial as they are in men – if the procedure wasn't as costly.

In the long corridor leading up to the boardroom, she ran into Rambo. His downcast eyes and his spiritless demeanour mirrored her own apprehensions. *At least today, there will be good food to eat,* she consoled herself.

CFC had never really served an all-you-can-eat buffet or even a formal sit-down lunch at any of their events. Sethji preferred oily, thick-crusted samosas with minimal filling, chicken lollipops made from emaciated chickens, and stale chutney sandwiches as pass-arounds. *Who could eat a full meal after that*? he reasoned. But today she was hopeful of something more than heavy Indian hors d'oeuvres. She was even optimistic of a main course. After all, *Avanti* was coming.

Walking through the open large double doors, her eyes were immediately drawn to the elaborate table arrangement. The set-up had the trademark bearing of La Maison, the celebrated French restaurant in Mumbai. Sethji had pulled out all the stops to impress Avanti!

After their customary greetings, Sethji and Rambo took their positions at the table. Like chess pieces, they placed themselves in their ordained spaces as per their ranking. Sethji presided at the top of the table with Rambo to his right. Megh was led by the hostess to the far end of the table, the vacant seats in between keeping her at an arm's length.

"Megh, thank you for joining us today," Sethji said cheerfully. "You are Avanti's sister-in-law, so when she decided to pay us a visit, I thought to myself, why not invite you as well. After all, very soon, you will be our relative too!"

Megh smiled and muttered a weak thank you. Megh fielded Sethji's questions on the Divine project while they waited for Avanti. Finally, after a long wait, when the hostess had just served the wine and the main course, Avanti sashayed through the tall doors in her six-inch Louboutin heels.

"Gosh! You won't believe what just happened," she exclaimed.

"Someone in your reception actually asked me who *I* was and who I intended to meet," she said, bending low to cheek-kiss everyone in the room, including Megh.

"Not their fault, you must come often," smiled Sethji.

"You are right, but still, the staff should know who their boss is marrying," she said, pouting for effect. "I think she was Rambo's PA. Skinny with hair so scanty that you could see her scalp. Eesh!" she shuddered at her own description.

"What was her name again?"

"Eliza," Sethji responded.

"Yes, that one. Dad, I think post marriage, I will start coming to the office more often. Your staff definitely needs help with some customer service training."

"Done, beta! I will even sort out a cabin for you, even better than mine."

Megh glanced at Rambo, who continued to stab his Veal Scaloppini listlessly.

"By the way, Megh, what do make of Surya's death?" Avanti asked, bluntly. "You know, Surya was *her* boss," Avanti pointed at Megh, "but *my* friend."

"Really? I thought you knew him through Megh," Sethji said, surprised.

"It was the other way around actually. She got to know Surya through us. She has a good wingman," Avanti said as she cut into her medium-rare steak.

"What do you mean?"

"Aadi got her that job at SGI and then, this job too. I know he called Rambo after Megh got fired from SGI, and the sweetheart that Rambo is, he couldn't refuse."

Megh felt her cheeks go red. Looking at her food, she realized that her fate was not much different from the untouched roast that was on her plate. Except she was the sacrificial lamb on slaughter today.

"Someone or the other always makes the introductions," Megh said, sipping her wine to control the fluctuation of tone in her voice, "nothing wrong if that happens to be my husband. Like how you know most of the cricketers because of *your* fiancé, and Sethji."

She glanced at Rambo. *Did she see a flicker of a smile before it disappeared in a flash?* He was now shoving big chunks of the veal down his throat. She would never know.

"Yes, that is true," Sethji said, pleased with the acknowledgment. "That reminds me, don't you guys have to leave for the match soon?"

"There is still time," Avanti said, glancing at her watch. "Maybe it's not such a good idea to take me to meet the team. You do know most of them love to ogle at me, right?" she said, throwing her head back and laughing.

"Oh, they can't help it! Nobody can keep their eyes away from a woman when her breasts are this plump and her hips this rounded!" Sethji replied, laughing heartily.

The crude sentence made Megh nauseous.

The intercom buzzed; it was Eliza.

"Sir, the police are here to talk about Surya Jain's death."

Megh stiffened. She felt Sethji's glare on her. "Make them wait in the lobby. Megh will be down in a minute."

"Sir, they are on their way up. They want to speak with you and Rambo."

Chapter 26
Imperial Towers II

Mumbai, 25th June 2016

Walking through the open double doors leading to CFC's conference room, Shreyas noticed a lonely cloche on one of the tables. They had interrupted a lunch party. He surveyed the room and detected a couple seated at opposite ends of a loveseat. Shreyas' eyes were drawn immediately to the attractive woman, her skimpy red skirt revealing her toned, bronzed legs. On catching his gaze, the woman lifted the skirt hem higher, much higher. Shreyas immediately looked away.

"To what do we owe this visit, officers?" said a short man from a dark velvet chair etched with golden enamel.

"Tulsidas Tekchand?" Hasan asked.

"Yes. But everyone calls me Sethji."

"Reema, your daughter, had an affair with Rajvir Jain," Hasan stated, coming to the point as usual.

"Yes, that unfortunate incident happened a long time ago. What about it?" Sethji answered stiffly.

"We have reason to believe that you might be behind Surya's death"

"How preposterous!" exclaimed the beautiful woman.

"And who are you?" Hasan asked.

"I am Avanti, and this is my fiancé, Rambo," she said, pointing to the man bundled in an expensive three-piece suit.

"How dare you speak to my father-in-law like that?" she added.

"Can you tell us more about the Reema and Rajvir debacle?" Hasan asked her, amused. "Did you know that your fiancé had a sister who committed suicide?"

"No."

"Then I suggest you shut up."

He turned his gaze towards Sethji. "Sethji, where were you on the night of Surya's death between 8 and 11 p.m.?"

"In my house."

"Can someone verify this?"

"My wife, my house staff, and my driver."

"And *Rambo*," Hasan was tickled by his name, "*the* fiancé of this beautiful prattler, where were you?"

"I don't remember," Rambo replied meekly.

"Is that so? But I read an article that said you forget nothing," Hasan asked, feigning a look of marvel on his face. "You don't remember, or you don't want to tell us?" Hasan persisted.

Rambo stared at his feet. The silence agitated Hasan.

"Why do you have gloves on?"

Rambo was dumbstruck by the sudden question.

"I… I… I wear them as I suffer from OCD that terrifies me from getting contaminated by germs."

"How about you tell me if those were the same gloves you wore the day you pushed Surya off the terrace?"

"What nonsense!" Avanti bellowed. "Rambo can never do such a thing, and that too to my friend Surya."

"Oh, interesting!" mused Hasan. "So Surya was your friend?"

"Yes, my brother Aadi and I had known him for years," Avanti haughtily lifted her chin.

"Aadi? So, Megh also knew Surya before she started working at SGI?"

"I don't know about that, but my brother got her that job."

"When did you last meet with Surya?"

"It's been a few years."

"You could have set it up for Rambo to meet Surya. He had the perfect motive, the means, and the ability to commit the crime," Hasan declared, clasping his hands together.

"Nothing of that sort happened," Rambo finally interrupted.

"Then why can't you tell us where you were?"

"Fuck this! He is too shy to say it in front of his father. He was with me, in my house, the entire night. It's okay, honey," she said, patting Rambo's hand.

"Can anyone else in your house corroborate this for us?" Hasan spoke.

"I had given the staff a day off, so no one really. But maybe the watchman saw him with me in the car? And of course, the CCTV may not have caught his face, but it will surely show that I walked in with him," Avanti answered confidently.

Sethji was relieved. He knew Rambo was not with her that evening. *What was Rambo trying to hide?*

"Sir, you think they could have done it?" Shreyas asked as soon as they were in the building elevator.

"Can't say, I want to see the CCTV footage of Avanti's building and check their alibis," Hasan said. "And this Aadi Wadhwa seems to be everywhere. We need to pay him a visit," he said thoughtfully.

Urvashi sniggered. "So now you have a new theory involving this Aadi. Our famous Officer Hasan is going around in circles to find a murderer in a case that's increasingly beginning to look like an accident. But how else will he redeem himself after he botched up the Sreelatha case, passing off a murder as an accident?" she retorted in contempt.

"I am just doing my investigation, but why are you in such a hurry to close it?" he asked her calmly.

"I don't want to waste my time on an old story that has no relevance to this case. There is too much paperwork piling up in the office."

"Spoken like a true bureaucrat. Since you find the investigation a waste of time, why don't you do the filing?" he said, winking at Shreyas.

"And Shreyas, you can accompany me," he added, the finality in his voice was undisputed.

Chapter 27
Mumbai Musketeers

Mumbai, 25th June 2016

The white Mercedes hiccupped a little at the small exit and then gathered speed on its way to Wankhede Stadium. Rambo had made sure that he had taken enough arsenal for the onward journey. He strategically placed a bound folder and a few company journals between him and his fiancée as station guards to discourage any conversation.

"Driver, can you turn up the AC please?" Avanti said, picking up one of Rambo's journals and fanning herself with it. "I like the temperature at nineteen degrees. Please make sure you make a note of it and remember it like forever."

Rambo noticed how she emphasised 'forever.'

"Sure, madam."

"Also, no Hindi music. Gosh Rambo! Haven't you taught your staff anything?"

This is a rhetorical question; I don't need to answer. Rambo told himself. So far so good. He tried to concentrate on the file in his hand, but his mind kept going back to Eliza. He wasn't sure why he had felt hurt when Avanti had spoken condescendingly about Eliza. Usually, he was very good at staying out of other people's business, but he wanted to meddle in Eliza's affairs. It was a strange feeling, something he had not experienced before.

"So where were *you* that night?" Avanti asked; this time, emphasising the you.

"I had a meeting with an environmentalist for the Divine project. I didn't want to say anything in front of Sethji; he would have been furious," he answered calmly. He was expecting the question.

"Environmentalist? I am sure Megh must have suggested it. Please don't fall for Megh and her stupid ideas."

"I think it is a brilliant idea. CFC will be the first to have locally, mass-produced, fair-trade chocolate in India."

"Ethical diamond, certified coffee, fair-trade chocolate – I think it is too much. All these are just ways to make consumers pay more. Why?" she ranted.

Rambo considered the question and decided again that she didn't want an answer.

After a short ride, the car came to a halt in the 'For Members Only' portico at the Wankhede Stadium.

Rambo disembarked, but Avanti continued to be seated. She said something to the driver, and he quickly jumped out of the car and opened the door for her. She moved towards the Players arena.

"Not there," Rambo said, "the team is going to meet us at the VIP lounge."

"You go ahead. I will join you in five minutes," she said.

In the lounge, Rambo ordered a Perrier and began to relax. Watching cricket was one of the most cathartic activities for him. He had little interest in the child's play of bat and ball, but he revelled in the prolific statistics, the unlikely odds, and the endless possibilities of the game.

Some of the Mumbai Musketeers' players started trickling in to meet with him. They were pumped about the upcoming series and assured him that they would lift the cup once again for the franchise. Their energy and optimism was contagious.

Looking for a bathroom, he headed to the nearest one, but it was closed for cleaning.

He decided to go to the player's arena, which was not too far away. He headed straight for the stalls. Inside the stall, after sanitising the bathroom seat, he was so absorbed in urinating that it was a while before he heard faint sounds as if someone was murmuring something in the adjoining stall. It was a woman. She was calling out Subu's name repeatedly. A man grunted rhythmically, a loud guttural grunt and the woman moaned in pleasure. Suddenly the noises stopped.

So did Rambo's pee.

There was a shuffling sound, a faucet running, and the clicking of heels. He recognised the cadence of the heels, the hard and fast clacking, always in a hurry with zero downtime in between. They belonged to Avanti. Suddenly he crouched on his seat, pulled out his phone and dialled her number. He needed to be sure. After a long pause, a phone started ringing.

"Shit, I have to run; my fatheaded fiancé is looking for me. Asshole can't even find words in his mouth to talk to someone."

"He is not that bad," the male voice countered.

"Oh, come on! The man is a dork. Oh, let me go, Subu!"

"Please tell me when you are going to meet me next?"

"Whenever."

"I want to fuck you on the day of your wedding."

"Oh baby, you know we will!" she emphasised 'will'

Rambo heard the heels clacking again, hard and fast before they faded away.

Chapter 28
Urvashi

Mumbai, 27th June 2016

Urvashi had ticked 'fair-skinned' on the matchmaking portal, and sitting in the outdoor seating at Café Day wearing a bright yellow dupatta, she felt fair-skinned. Her date today was with a businessman. He had ticked fair-skinned, too, which he was, but he was also balding and overweight.

Their conversation, for some reason, revolved mostly around his work. She was glad he wasn't asking her about her work. She hated talking about it; she also hated doing it.

"Do you like to travel?" he asked.

"Yes." She smiled a tight-lipped, polite smile. She had been practicing that smile. It made her appear coy, the one ingredient that reduced the acidity of being a female cop.

Her phone began to ring. It was Baba. She ignored it.

He called again.

"You should get it. You are a cop, it might be important," her date said, concerned.

"Where are you?" Baba hollered as soon as she picked up. She was relieved she had moved a couple of tables away.

"In a meeting."

"With who, why are you not working on the SJ case?"

"Baba, I told you there is nothing more to do, but that Hasan is a maniac. He is obsessed with the D'sire chocolate scandal. You told me to let him take the lead, so I am letting him do his thing."

"I also told you to tag along, you must be seen! How will you ever get promoted if you are not at work!" he reprimanded her loudly.

"I am not going to waste my time."

"You are making me very angry, Urvashi. Stop wasting your time meeting men, especially not when you should be on duty! That Hasan is at Aadi's office. Go and do your job!" he hollered again.

"Okay," she responded calmly before hanging up.

She headed back to her table.

"Was that an important call? It's okay if you have to leave," her date said, smiling earnestly.

She returned his smile. "Nothing important, just routine. So what were you saying?" she said as she sipped her mocha.

Chapter 29
Husbands

Mumbai, 27th June 2016

Entering through the glass doors of Aadi's office, they were astounded by the juxtaposition of cutting-edge, clean, contemporary lines with atypical antique-looking furniture. Along with luxurious hand-crafted pieces, the office also housed a lot of modern art and large floor-to-ceiling windows that brought in the magnificent ocean right up to the office cabin. Shreyas wondered how anybody could work in such a distracting environment.

"Let me know if I can help you with anything," the receptionist said, guiding them to a high-back sofa in the waiting area.

"Can we get some coffee?" Shreyas requested. His palate, like his career, was advancing and accumulating some urban finesse.

"Of course." She smiled and pointed to a console. "That's our beverage bar. Please help yourself."

"What bar? I only know a beer bar," he muttered at her immediate dismissal.

"And dance bar?" Hasan chimed in, laughing.

"*No re baba,*" Shreyas replied, tugging his ear lobes with his fingers and staving himself from such grave sins.

They headed over to the beverage bar.

Shreyas hesitantly moved closer to the coffee machine. He picked a tiny cup, hoping not to come across as greedy, and hit a button cautiously. The machine started with a small trickle, but by midstream, it had gained enough momentum and was about to spill over when a tempered arm reached over his shoulders and swapped the cups.

"That cup is for an espresso. Let me get that," Aadi said.

Holding their cups, he led them to his cabin – the largest in the office.

"To what do I owe this visit?" Aadi asked, smiling warmly.

"Where were you on the night of Surya's death?"

"I was out of the country. I was at the airport when I heard the news."

"Your sister mentioned that you and Surya were friends."

"We had common friends."

"I believe you got your wife Megh her job with SGI," Hasan continued.

"Not really, she would have gotten it anyway."

"What do you mean?"

Aadi took a sip from his coffee before he began. "I met Megh at a party that Avanti had thrown at Emporis. After the party, I went to drop her home, and in the car, she told me about her upcoming interview with SGI. I had been out of the country for very long. I didn't know then that SGI was owned by the Jains.

"I vividly remember her talking about this idea for a chocolate that she was so keen on discussing with them. I was intrigued by her, so I offered to drive her to her interview. But I was jet-lagged and fell asleep on the wheel and the car crashed into a tree. We both sustained minor injuries, but she was furious that she had missed the interview," he laughed before continuing again. "She was mad at me, that my carelessness had cost her – 'a middle-class girl' in her words – her dreams.

"I wanted to make up to her. When I learnt that SGI belonged to the Jains, and that Surya was active in the business, I called him and helped her reschedule her interview. A week later, she got the offer. She had to, that girl was dreaming of making that chocolate for I don't know how many years."

"You moved back to India for her. You must have fallen hard," Hasan said.

"I was contemplating that move anyway, but yes," Aadi nodded. "She felt alive, and she spoke her mind. She was different from all the other women I had dated."

"How were Megh's relations with Surya?"

"Regular, like a co-worker's."

"Maybe they were more than co-workers…, but you just didn't want to see it?"

"I am a lawyer, sir. I see things I shouldn't be seeing."

"That is the problem. Sometimes, the lawyers and the police – experts that they are at reading between the lines – miss out on entire chapters when it comes to their own lives," Hasan petered out.

Shreyas was uneasy. *Was Hasan talking about his own experience?*

"Well, thank you for your wisdom, are we done here?" Aadi broke off Shreyas' trail of thought.

"Have you ever asked her? Middle-class girl and yet partying till so late in the night before her dream job interview? Ask her, my friend, ask her." Hasan was relentless.

"I think you have crossed a line now," Aadi's anger was boiling over.

"Have I? I think your wife is a gold digger. Her aim was always to get to Surya, the biggest fish... That was why she was so mad when you crashed the car. But then she realised she could have both – you as the husband and he as the boyfriend – double bonanza!"

"Enough! Get out of my office right now!" Aadi was furious.

Hasan chuckled as he walked out of the office with Shreyas.

Chapter 30
The Sardar Police Station

Mumbai, 27th June 2016

It was easy for Shreyas to guess that Hasan was having a good day as he was playing imaginary cricket. The lotus-shaped paperweight was his mock cricket ball, and Hasan was going through the motions of bowling one of Jasprit Bumrah's fiery yorkers as if he was about to win the cup for India.

Urvashi suddenly stormed into the station, peeling off her dupatta and dumping her bag on the table. It was equally easy for Shreyas to guess she was having a bad day. He had overheard two women constables discuss how the Café Day date had also ended in a rejection.

"Who the fuck took my mosquito net?" she screamed.

With all its arsenal and intelligence, the Sardar police station still couldn't defend itself against the treacherous mosquitoes and depended on the mosquito meshes velcroed on the windows to do the job. Shreyas looked at the exposed window in Urvashi's cabin; someone had nicked hers. He quickly peeled off one from a nearby window and offered it to her.

"So, what did you guys uncover at your investigation?" Urvashi asked, fanning herself with a file.

"That, I have been right all along. There seems to be a love angle here. Surya and Megh, and Aadi, the cuckold," Hasan said triumphantly. "By the way, where were you?"

"I don't owe you an explanation. I refuse to fall for your love angle theories, just because of what happened with your wife!" She was frothing with anger.

"Urvashi ma'am, you don't need to get personal," Shreyas interjected.

"Oh, shut up, you little puppy! You like being his doormat, don't you!? Always at his beck and ca—"

"You bitch, how dare you talk about my wife?" Hasan roared.

"Oh, the truth hurts, does it? And the truth is that you couldn't keep her happy; that's why she left you!"

Hasan instinctively hurled the paperweight in his hand at Urvashi. It hit her head before dropping to the ground with a dull thud. A pool of blood stained her yellow suit, dyeing it a rusty orange.

Chapter 31
Aadi

Sitting in his balcony, Aadi was alone. Megh had messaged him that she was going to be working late again. This was becoming a pattern. He felt neglected. He poured himself his Oban, adding ice until his glass was full to the brim. He liked his whiskey on the rocks, and Megh liked it neat. *I don't tolerate adulteration*; she had said to him when they were dating, not even in my alcohol. He had laughed at the comment then. He could only offer a wry smile now.

He remembered the day in the hospital when he had sat by her bedside, waiting for her to gain consciousness. The doctors had assured him that it was a minor head concussion, that she would be fine, but he had felt a deep fear of losing a loved one; it was weird as he had known her for less than twelve hours.

Her hair dishevelled, her mascara smudged, and her lipstick smeared, he had seen a defiant Megh glare at him when she gained consciousness. That face was imprinted in his memory, and it always made him smile. That's what his daughter would look like when she would throw a tantrum. But Megh had changed over the years. The reality was, since Surya's death, there had been no sex and no baby talk. It was as if his sight repulsed her. Aadi couldn't stop himself from rewinding the afternoon's conversation with Hasan in his head. *Did she feel something for Surya? Was there something between the two of them?*

Suddenly an image flashed in front of his eyes.

It was the night when he first met her. Megh had just delivered her sermon on the G-spot. She was blowing smoke in a guy's face, who had pulled her to the dance floor once again and was revolving around with her. He seemed familiar. Was that Surya?

Chapter 32
Hasan

On some occasions, when doom had secretly slipped on its gloves and knocked someone out, he had been a silent bystander. He had even moved out of the way, sometimes, and in that, he had been a colluder, but he had never been the perpetrator of doom. Today, he felt like one. The guilt was still standing, unwavering, and resolute in its intentions. Only a joint could help. After finishing one, he called Shreyas.

"Hello?" a tired voice replied.

"Shreyas, did I wake you up?"

"No problem, sir."

"How is Urvashi?"

"Urvashi madam has just reached home from the hospital, after getting stitches. "

"'Sir," he paused, "what you did was not correct. I think you should apologise."

"Yes, text me her address."

"Sir, I mean over the phone, please don't go there!" Shreyas panicked.

"No, I will not go; I just want to send her some flowers."

As soon as he received Shreyas' text, Hasan picked his car keys and headed out.

It was three o'clock at night when he sped through the yawning roads of Mumbai and arrived at Urvashi's building.

He vaulted up four flights of stairs and rang the doorbell. He was still panting when an old man seated in his wheelchair, his urine bag in tow, opened the door. His bleary eyes searched Hasan's face. He suddenly shouted, "You rascal!" in his frail voice. "How dare you?"

"Sir, I have come to apologise. Can I please come in?"

"No!" a cold stern female voice replied.

Urvashi was lying on a single bed with a thick bandage wrapped around her head. A plate of uneaten food was kept on top of a pile of old newspapers. Reluctantly, the old man allowed Hasan in, and wheeled himself away to the other side of the room, where he heaved himself to his feet and hobbled towards the TV-facing couch. Hasan realised that the places had been swapped. The father had assigned his injured daughter the only bed in the house.

"I am sorry," Hasan said, sincerely. "My intention was not to hurt you."

"It doesn't matter," she sighed. "I don't want to work with you. I have already lodged a complaint."

"Please, Urvashi. It will ruin my career."

"That's what you deserve. And if you stay here any longer, I will call the commissioner."

Hasan lingered for a few moments and offered a weak goodbye that remained unrequited before shutting the door behind him.

Back in the car, he tried to focus on a single thought – something, anything, but they were running, always ahead of him, always leading him into places where he didn't want to go. *Why don't I just finish everything off at once? I should just press the accelerator and drive off the road. At least it will be an honourable death.*

With trembling fingers, he rolled another joint and took a drag.

His phone buzzed. It was a WhatsApp from Abu.

Where are you?

He typed back, *I am out.*

Next, he read Abu's standard line. *Are you busy?*

Tears welled up in his eyes. Poor Abu, he was still so proud of his son. His mind flashed an image of a much older-looking Abu burying his son's mangled body.

He pulled up on the side, and replied. *Go to sleep, don't worry about me. I will see you in the morning.*

After a couple of drags, Hasan started driving again. Looking around, he realised that he wasn't far from the Dadar Parsi Colony.

"What are you doing here? At this time of the night?" Dr Poonawala's plump face spilled through the grill of the main door.

"I need to talk to you. It's urgent...please," Hasan implored.

"How did you even find me?"

"I am with the police, remember!"

"You do know these sort of unannounced visits are not allowed. It's an invasion of my privacy. Go home; I will see you tomorrow morning, during office hours," he replied sternly.

"I attacked a woman... with my bare hands," Hasan stared at his upturned palms.

"What!?"

"I hit Urvashi."

Wrapping his robe tighter, Dr Poonawala opened the latch to his door. "You better come in," he said, resigning himself to his fate.

Inside the Parsi home, Hasan told his story in complete honesty.

"I can't believe I attacked a woman," Hasan was woeful. "I don't think I know myself anymore. No wonder people think that I am some misogynist."

"Are you? Do you hate women?" Dr Poonawala gently enquired.

"Only the ones who have been close to me," he mumbled. Hasan's guard was down.

"Like?"

"My mother and my wife. They both left me."

"Have you tried reaching out to them? Understanding why they left is an important part of the healing process."

"No."

"What happened with your wife?"

"I caught her having an affair with my best friend – in my own bedroom. They had hidden it from me for a very long time," Hasan answered matter-of-factly.

"Then it's only natural that you feel this way towards certain women."

"It's somehow the same picture," Hasan said blankly.

"What picture?"

"The picture that was taken at D'sire's success party; Megh is standing with her hand loosely hanging around Surya. My wife…" he paused. "I have a picture from one of our Eid parties, and Salma, is also standing like this with…" his voice trailed off.

It was a while before he spoke again.

"That picture makes my blood boil," he continued. "I know there is no connection, but every time I see Megh's face, I am sure she is hiding a crime behind it. But to hit someone, I must be turning into a monster." He pulled out his glasses and rubbed the indents on the bridge of his nose.

"Why do you do that?"

"Do what?"

"That," he said, pointing to his nose. "Can you see the marks on your nose?"

"Obviously, I can't."

"But you know they are there. What you have developed against women is just like that indent. It's there; it's an implicit bias that you have been harbouring for years," he explained.

"At least now you are aware of your bias. It may not disappear completely, but it surely will become less. Things will surely change. You need to build empathy – brick by brick – to feel human again."

"We all are monsters; at least you know which one you are," he added as an afterthought, smiling kindly at him.

They sat in silence for a few minutes before Hasan spoke again.

"Doctor, maybe you should only practice during the night. Somehow you make more sense," Hasan said as he walked towards the stairs.

Chapter 33
Emporis Apartments

Mumbai, 28th June 2016

Hasan parked his car at the foot of Pali Hill and decided to walk his way up to Emporis. He could use the exercise. He pulled out his glasses, wiped the lenses, and rubbed the indents on his nose thoroughly. The sky seemed clearer, as if the veneer of dust that had accumulated over decades had been wiped off.

Jazz, the housemaid, opened the door and let him in.

"Didi, the police is here for you."

"Yes, officer. What can I do for you?" Megh asked, gliding in with a glass of wine in one hand and a book in the other.

"I want to listen to your side of the story, what *you* have to say."

"That," she gulped down her drink and said, "is the sexiest thing a man can say to a woman."

"Huh?" he said, gruffly.

"That you want to listen to me – even if it is as part of an interrogation," she said, smiling at him as she led the way into her living room.

"What happened the day you got fired from the company?"

"That is a long story. I suggest you join me for a drink." Megh pulled out a chilled Pinot Grigio from the wine cooler, offered him a glass and refilled hers. He took it without any hesitation.

"I remember that day vividly. It was a week after the Agra party. We were back in our offices when Chana buzzed me that MJ had called an urgent board meeting. I could sense the tension as soon as I entered the conference room. MJ was furious about the complaint that stated that our chocolate, D'sire, contained ADR. I was shocked. I tried to explain that we were being framed, but I was humiliated and fired in front of everyone. I was the perfect scapegoat. I was very upset, especially with Surya, as he said nothing in front of his grandfather and his father.

"Later that day, Surya approached me and said he was sure it was not me; that he trusted me.

"Instead, he said he thought it was Toni. He convinced the board to set up an internal investigation that had to present its findings in seventy-two hours. I doubted Toni's involvement because this kind of stuff needed technical knowledge, which Toni lacked. I suspected Ali; he was the only one who knew how to do something like this. His sudden disappearance, followed by his resignation from Nigeria, was suspicious. He was uncontactable. Surya agreed that something was fishy. We wanted to dig deeper, so we searched Ali's workstation. We checked his computer and found that all the data had been wiped clean. There was nothing on it. Our IT specialist confirmed that someone had manually deleted the data.

"You mean someone had cleaned everything from Ali's computer *after* he had left for Nigeria?"

"Yes."

"Did you check the CCTV footage to see who it was?"

"We did. It took us some time to get our hands on it, but what we found was unthinkable. We found footage of Ashok deleting everything from Ali's computer."

"Ashok? As in Surya's father?"

"Yes, but by then, the internal investigation report was out, and it showed Toni's signatures on the purchase of ADR. That news leaked, and Toni, who was at our milk factory in Karnataka, was lynched, and he died."

"So you were free?"

"I was still fired, but my neck was no longer on the line. Nothing made sense. Why would Ashok delete everything from Ali's computer? So I pestered Surya to confront him."

"That means you were still in touch with Surya. Didn't your previous statements to the police say that you didn't meet him after you were fired?"

"This was just maybe a week or so after getting fired. I wanted to get to the bottom of the mess."

"What happened? Do you know if Surya confronted his father?"

"Yes, he did. At first, Ashok denied everything. Then Surya showed him the CCTV footage, and Ashok finally confessed. He said that he had always felt like a failure; he had never been able to measure up to his father's expectations, and he was worried Surya would fail too. He wanted to ensure that Surya's project was a hit. Ali had convinced Ashok that ADR would make D'sire a better-tasting chocolate, and Ashok had given him the green signal."

"Then how come Toni's signatures were on it?"

"I asked Surya the same question, but he didn't care. He told me to forget about it as I was acquitted, Toni was dead, and that story had become stale."

"Why didn't you say anything? Tell everyone about Ashok?"

"There was a report that said Toni had done it. Who would believe me? I would come off looking like a shit-stirrer, making noise for cheap publicity."

Hasan sat quietly, trying to process all the information.

"You don't like me, right?" Megh suddenly asked him.

"Yes," he replied with a smile.

"Then why have you come here to listen to me?"

He removed his glasses and rubbed the bridges of his nose. "To be able to see you differently."

"Do you know how I see myself?" she asked him. He sensed that she was a little drunk.

"No."

"I see myself as an *Ardhanarishvara*."

"A what?"

"It is a combination of three words: *Ardha*, *Nari*, and *Ishwara*, which mean half, woman and lord, respectively. A composite androgynous form of the Hindu deities Shiva and Parvati, the Ardhanarishvara is depicted as half-male and half-female, equally split down the middle. A human being is not a pure unisexual organism. Each human organism bears the potentiality of both male and female sex. Ardhanarishvara is an example of androgyny in Indian mythology. In 1832, when Samuel Taylor Coleridge, the celebrated philosopher, wrote that *'a great mind must be androgynous'*, this is what he was talking about."

"But male and female are the very first categories of experiences into which we are placed as new-borns," Hasan countered.

"Yes, these distinctions continue to shape society's expectations of us throughout our lives, but the most fertile mental and spiritual landscape is one where there is ample cross-pollination between the two."

"So, you are saying that we should not see a boy as a boy and a girl as a girl?" he asked.

"Of course, when we need to reproduce or fornicate, we must, but maybe at other times, we can all just be fellow androgynous beings?"

"See each other as just humans, you mean? With no distinction of gender?" he elaborated his thoughts slowly.

"Exactly! Male, female, how does it matter?" she said, gulping down the last of her drink.

They shared the silence for a while.

"Anyway, will this be all?"

"Yes, this will be all," Hasan said. He collected his car keys and left.

Chapter 34
The Sardar Police Station

Mumbai, 29th June 2016

Though Hasan had been AWOL for the entire day, his 'attack' on Urvashi had been a part of every conversation, including those amongst cellmates. Shreyas let out a sigh of relief when Hasan finally reported to duty.

"Shreyas, my friend, how are you?" Hasan asked brightly

"I am well, sir. You seem to be well too.'"

"I am indeed," Hasan replied. "I just got a massive lead."

"On which case?" Shreyas asked, his eyebrows furrowing.

"You will find out soon, just set up the interrogation room till I get my coffee."

Walking towards their makeshift kitchen, Shreyas noticed that as Hasan passed through the aisle, the animated stories brewing in the station before his arrival came to a grinding halt. Everyone suddenly went silent. It was as if he was emanating a terrifying gas that had choked everyone's voice. By the time he passed Urvashi's cabin, he had become deadly like Chernobyl.

Suddenly, Shreyas caught Ashok Jain walking in through the doors.

He couldn't believe Hasan had called Ashok in for interrogation!

Ashok sat with his shoulders pulled back and stared straight at Hasan with defiance. "Why have I been called in? And can you please hurry up? I have other matters to attend to."

"Other matters more important than the death of your son?"

"What do you mean?"

"I have got my hands on a CCTV recording," Hasan said, waving a pen drive at him. "It shows you deleting all the records on Ali's computer. Can you tell me more about that?"

Ashok stiffened. "I refuse to answer your question."

"You may, but the truth is…"

Just then, Shreyas felt his phone vibrate. It was the Commissioner of Police. Shreyas knew it was for Hasan and quickly handed it over to him.

"Why have you summoned Mr Ashok Jain to the station?"

Shreyas could hear the commissioner screaming. It seemed like the commissioner had taken a masterclass on brevity; he wasn't wasting any words.

"I am interrogating him for the SJ death case. I have a lead, sir – an important one," Hasan said, determinedly.

"For god's sake, Hasan! Have you completely lost it? First, you attack my senior police officer, then you call such an esteemed personality to the station. I have spoken with the lab. They found nothing suspicious and are releasing the body. The death was an accident. This case is closed. And Hasan, you are suspended."

Hasan paused as he watched Ashok, who had heard the commissioner, stand up to his full height, straighten his suit and march out right in front of him.

"Sir, how could nothing be found in his body?" he continued. We are sure he inhaled and ingested all kinds of stuff. Don't suspend me, sir. Please! We are very close to uncovering something. This is not an accident. Madam Sharda gave us a lead on CFC, and that Megh has no alibi about where she was that night. And now, I have a strong lead on Asho—" Hasan was cut midway by an even more livid commissioner.

"Stop this nonsense, right now! Urvashi called me and told me how Sharda ji didn't say anything about Sethji. I personally spoke with Sharda ji as well, and she said she would die before even thinking such thoughts. CFC is like family to them, and Sethji is like her own father!"

"Sir, you can ask Shreyas..." Hasan said, surprised. Urvashi had lied to her boss. It was a smart trick; there was no way Sharda was going to admit that she had divulged that piece of information. Urvashi had taken her revenge, and now he had been suspended. Again.

"Go home, Hasan," the commissioner said, with an exhausting apathy in his voice before hanging up.

Chapter 35
Abu

Mumbai, 30th June 2016

Hasan didn't recognise the man in the mirror wearing a green *pathaani* suit with gelled back hair and a pruned beard.

"Looking sharp," Abu said, catching him by surprise. "You have a date?" he asked.

"Yes."

"With who?"

"A corpse, I am going to a condolence."

"Oh, that Surya Jain case. Thank god the family got the body. Is the case closed?"

"Yes."

"Accident?"

Hasan nodded.

"The Jains are such a respectable family. I was sure that it was an accident. I am so glad you saw it too," his father added, sympathetically.

For a moment, Hasan wanted to tell his father about his suspension, about the politics within the police department, about the big bosses and corrupt peers, but he decided against it.

"Listen, Karim has made some biryani; why don't you eat a little? You used to love it."

Abu had visited *dargahs* to ward off the evil residing within his son and to seek forgiveness for his behaviour.

Clearly nothing had worked except that he had learned to stay out of his son's matters. He had never asked him why Salma left him or why he had been suspended from the Sreelatha case. Today, what was left of his relationship with his son was primal: An offering of biryani that he relished, an appeal to repair a bathroom leak, a plea to get *chaadar* for the dargah that ought to be offered – conversations around food, shelter, and clothing. Beyond all of humanity's collective wisdom, at the end of the day, like all other creatures, human beings were basically primal.

Hasan smiled warmly and said, "Okay."

Chapter 36
Condolence

Shreyas reconsidered the parking spot of his eight-year-old Bata shoes. Next to the line-up of branded footwear, they looked abandoned and needy. He moved them next to a pair of slippers with black gunk on the footbed, hoping that they felt comfort in each other's company, before hurrying inside the prayer hall.

"Why are *you* so late?" Hasan chided him as he saw him tripping in.

"I didn't know you were coming," Shreyas responded earnestly.

"Why not! I was the only guy wanting justice for Surya," Hasan said jokingly. But suddenly turning serious, he added, "I may be suspended, but it doesn't change the fact that I feel bad for the family, and that I want to offer my condolences. Anyway, the clash of the titans is about the begin. I am betting on that guy."

"What are you talking about?" Shreyas was confused.

"Look ahead."

Usually reserved for huge wedding receptions, the Hyatt hotel ballroom had been booked for the condolence and was full.

"The Mumbai family's pandit, and the Chavad clan's pandit, who has been flown in for this occasion, are seated right at the front. They must have been told to tread the

137

middle ground and take turns in conducting the ceremony," Hasan continued, pointing them out.

"Where is Urvashi ma'am?"

"Seated right at the front, with the commissioner. Megh and Aadi are here as well."

"Oh, this will be fun," Shreyas said, his voice trembling with excitement as he spotted Sethji walk in, with Rambo and Subu flanking him on either side. They were escorted right to the front of the line. Hands folded, in an unexpected gesture, Sethji touched MJ's feet, then Sharda touched Sethji's feet, and then Sethji and Ashok hugged tightly.

"*Saala*, I was the only *chutiya* around. The Wadhwas, the Tekchands, and the Jains have become one big happy family, Urvashi is hobnobbing with the big bosses, and I am the one who got suspended!"

Chapter 37
Rambo

L ying on his king-sized bed, Rambo furled and unfurled from one side to the other, trying to fall asleep. It had been a crazy day and his mind was restless. The day after Avanti's brief encounter with Eliza, Eliza had handed in her resignation. Rambo just couldn't imagine a life that didn't involve her. Elegant, organised and kind, Eliza was the human equivalent of Canada. Her sudden resignation had prompted him to understand that his dependency was more than just work-related; he was in love with her. In that instant, he had buzzed her on the intercom and said those three words, *'I love you'*. She had cried for a long time. They were tears of happiness, she had reassured him. Rambo had promised Eliza that he would talk to Sethji soon.

Chapter 38
Rambo

Mumbai, 2nd July 2016

Rambo arrived in Sethji's den at 7 a.m. sharp.
Sethji was reading the newspaper. Even in India, he read *The Malta Daily* every day. Sitting opposite his father, his knees pressing against each other, Rambo blurted, "I went with Avanti to meet the team at Wankhede."

"Yes, I know," Sethji replied as he continued to read the paper without a glance.

"There I found out something disturbing."

"What?" Sethji sighed and folded his paper neatly on the table.

"Avanti is having an affair with Subu."

"I know."

"Oh! And you are okay with it?" Rambo was puzzled.

"She is your fiancée. If she is happy with you, she will not go anywhere else."

"But she doesn't get me. I love Eliza; she gets me."

"Eliza is your PA, she gets paid to get you."

"But why are you so insistent on Avanti? You surely know that we are not compatible," he argued.

"She doesn't seem to have a problem with you; and for you, there couldn't be a better wife than her," Sethji declared. "She is the only one who can launch your career and steer it in the right direction. Get ready for your wedding. It's happening in four days." With that, Sethji went back to reading the paper.

He didn't intend to, but suddenly, Rambo remembered Reema. Unable to come to terms with her loss, he had archived her memory in a special place where he catalogued the traumatic experiences he wanted to forget, but today every little detail about her came gushing out. He remembered Sethji bribing officials to find out the truth. He remembered hearing that MJ could have saved her. He remembered Sethji's anger.

"What else can I expect from a man who hugged his own enemy? Yes, I saw how you behaved at Surya's condolence meet. You have joined hands with the same MJ who killed your daughter as you want their support in securing a government deal in Maldives where they are powerful," Rambo said bitterly. "You are a ruthless, conniving, hateful man who only thinks about profit!"

"Oh, shut up and spare me the sermon!" Sethji shut him down immediately. "Out of twenty-four hours, you are in the bathroom for eight hours; you are terrified to shake hands with anyone; you can't string a sentence intelligently, and *you* have the temerity to talk to me like that! Yes, I am ruthless and conniving, and you have lived your entire life on the profits that I have worked hard to amass. You have one day to decide. If you stay, I will know that you are willing to marry Avanti. If you leave, you are free to marry whoever you want."

Chapter 39
Revenge

Mumbai, 6th July 2016

Toads project their sticky tongues and swallow their prey wholly, especially the beetles. They are so quick in stuffing their prey down their gullets, that the beetles get no time to process this sudden attack. Just like the beetle, Eliza had been dumped and stuffed down the gullet by her boyfriend of one day in a matter of minutes. It had been business as usual at CFC. Rambo hadn't spoken to her at all after their brief call. Instead, Sethji had given her a raise and the additional responsibility of being the hostess-in-charge at the wedding. Eliza wondered if Sethji had made her stay back to ensure she would be tormented every minute for wanting to be Rambo's bride.

Even though the wedding was to be an intimate affair – just under a hundred guests – the hype around it was not. Themed around a caravan, the outdoor venue of The H Hotel was brimming with food trucks. A crew of over two hundred chefs had been flown down from all over the world. Especially for his bahu, Sethji had flown in the chef of a famous crepe station from Paris.

The walkway of the venue was created like a bazaar. Banjara dance troops, and traditional folk singers who had triumphed in the selection process were ready for their opening performances. Photo booth opportunities included close-ups with elephants and camels and a longshot with a computer generated imagery-made tiger.

Sethji wanted an unplugged wedding. The request, 'No photos or videos please' had been printed on the wedding invite. The guests were again reminded of the social media protocol upon entering the venue. Sethji, of course, had agreed to sell the wedding footage to a media conglomerate for a whopping price. What Sethji did not know was that the beetles consumed by toads could cause so much irritation in their attackers' stomachs that they forced many to regurgitate them. Eliza was one such beetle. She had instructed her stooges at the wedding to take pictures surreptitiously and post them on social media in real time. She was going to take her revenge digitally.

Chapter 40
Hasan

Mumbai, 6th July 2016

Hasan opened the cardboard box that had been delivered to his house. It contained the remnants of his short-lived stint at the Sardar police station. He pulled out the ill-famed paperweight and placed it gingerly by his window-sill. The naïve memento was still thanking him for his service. The remaining contents were mainly case-related papers, a worn-out belt that he had unleashed a few days ago post a heavy Indo-Chinese meal, and a manila envelope addressed to him from Roma, Surya'a PA @ SGI.

Before tearing it open, he inspected the flap to ensure that it had not been tampered with and then pulled out its sole occupant – a letterhead bearing a list of names of people Surya had met the week leading up to his death. A name at the very bottom caught his eye.

Avanti Wadhwa.

He dialled Shreyas immediately.

"Sir, how are you doing?" Shreyas asked, the concern ringing through his voice.

"Shreyas, I need a favour."

"Anything, sir."

"I have the names of all the people Surya met before he died."

"Was that what it was in the sealed envelope? I just put it along with all your other belongings."

"Avanti met with him," Hasan stated, getting straight to the point.

"Oh, that's a googly! She didn't mention it. In fact, she said it'd been a few years since she had met with him."

"Find out ASAP!"

"It's her wedding today, sir! I don't know what I can do."

"There could be a murderer getting away, and all you have to say is that *'it's her wedding day today'*?" Hasan retorted sarcastically.

"I will try, sir," Shreyas hung up and immediately felt a piercing gaze bearing him down. It was Urvashi.

"He wants me to…"

"I heard what he wants," she interjected. "Do it!" she commanded.

"What?" Shreyas asked, confused.

"Do it, but report the findings to me! You will not call him."

"Yes ma'am."

Chapter 41
Wedding

Mumbai, 6th July 2016

A red Pajero followed by Aadi's blue BMW coughed and clamoured as it was intercepted by a liveried hand at the security booth of The H Hotel in Juhu, Mumbai. An officer strode towards the car and scanned the wedding card handed by the driver that read: *Avanti weds Rammeher.*

He tapped on the window, indicating that it be rolled down completely.

"You here for the wedding?"

"Yes, sir."

"Are you the driver?"

"Yes sir," Munna replied dejectedly. The officer had, in an instant, scratched through the layers of Munna's white suit, the extra crisp gelled hair, and the fake gold-plated watch to see his profession that was perhaps imprinted on his soul.

Munna was about to forewarn his fellow travel companions that they may undergo the same class-based grilling, but before he could do anything, the officer stuck his head through the window and scrutinised them.

His eyes were greeted by a skittish man seated in the passenger seat and two ladies sitting in the back, fidgeting with the hems of their colourful dupattas. *Damn! There is too much nervous energy inside the car. He will know we are all domestic helpers and will try to stop us from entering his hotel. His*

146

ilk doesn't care that we have been in Avanti baby's service our entire lives, Munna thought to himself.

"You think a card is enough to get you jokers entry into this wedding?" The officer scoffed. The halo of bureaucracy emitted its glow even more brightly.

Before Munna could say anything, Megh, who had been waiting outside the lobby as a part of the reception party, recognised the car and called out to the security.

"Any problem, officer? I am Megh; it's my sister-in-law's wedding, and these are my guests."

"Nothing madam, just doing my duty!"

"Thank you," she responded, offering a namaste.

Tailing the Pajero, Aadi's car sailed through the security check with ease.

"Is that Megh in a saree?" a friend remarked from the backseat of his car. "She is looking so hot!"

Aadi looked at his wife. Draped in a black saree with a bold blouse highlighting her clavicle, she was sharing a light moment with her colleagues from CFC. She did look stunning. He halted the car right in front of her, almost as if touching her feet for forgiveness.

"We really are late! Get ready to defend me," he said to no one in particular as Megh glared at him.

"We don't come between husband and wife!" his co-passenger replied.

"How can you be late *today*?" Megh chided.

"One can only be so early to an Indian wedding, never late," Aadi chuckled as he unfurled his long limbs and battled it out with his aquiline-nosed aristocratic *mojris*. He jumped out of his car and kissed his wife. A gloss, not a deep kiss.

"Well, *you* can do anything, Aadi," she said, her tone laced with sarcasm.

"That is indeed true," he laughed.

"We have a situation."

"What?" he said, putting his arm around her shoulder.

"The groom is refusing to sit on the mare for his *baraat*."

"So cancel the baraat. Simple."

"The pandit is saying it's *apshagun*."

"For him it most definitely must be, his *baksheesh* from that function is under threat," Aadi said. "Hang on! Isn't Avanti also staying in this hotel?"

"Yes, thank god, at least you know something about your only sister's wedding.

"So baraat is from his room to hers?"

"Something like that. The baraat was to leave from one gate and return through the other in thirty minutes."

"I still can't believe it. Avanti agreed to marry *Rambo* after breaking up with Subu, who she dumped because he didn't make it to India's 11. Look now, he is the captain of this new T20 team."

"And she is the new owner of the team."

"What? How?"

"How can you not know this, Aadi? CFC owns Mumbai Musketeers. It's literally her team! Subu is the captain for this season of the league matches. Sethji will make sure he attends the wedding too."

"Oh shit!" Aadi exclaimed. "I just remembered that I have to give something to Avanti."

"What?"

He reached inside the pocket of his kurta and pulled out a jewellery box. As he opened it, their eyes were greeted by an elegant diamond choker.

"One of Cartier's finest!" Megh exclaimed, recognising the distinct pattern.

"It's my mom's necklace. Dad wanted Avanti to have it. I will be back soon," he said, looking at her for approval.

She nodded as he set off.

It was a long walk towards the hotel's residential tower. Aadi realised how little he knew about his sister. Especially since she had moved out and lived alone. He always knew his sister Avanti Wadhwa was dazzling. She stunned people. That was her superpower. Her unblinking eyes and her hypnotic smile made it impossible for anyone not to be lured. It was as if she had wagered a bet with herself that at all times, only she must be the cynosure of all eyes. And she did whatever it took to win that bet – drugs, sex, naked photos, whatever.

The Wadhwa parents had thought that parcelling off their dazzling daughter to schools run by nuns that stipulated and monitored the length of school skirts and served eggs only on Sundays would solve the problem. But she dazzled them so much that she was expelled from two schools before finally arriving at the third.

Between boarding schools and mismatched holidays, Aadi didn't see her much; and for the brief period that they inhabited the same house, he felt he didn't know her at all. They shared genes and a last name, but no memories or stories.

Today, at the threshold of her wedding, he hoped that by giving her their mom's necklace, he could make a special memory. Feeling the ridges of the box in his pocket with his hand, he knocked firmly on her room door. There was no response.

He knocked harder. A shuffling sound, a click of the lock, and Avanti opened with the door-chain firmly in place.

"What are you doing here?" she asked, bundled in a bathrobe.

"Can I come in?"

"No," her voice was decisive. "I am getting ready."

Aadi heard a flush gurgle in the toilet.

"Who is in there?" he asked sharply.

"None of your business really, Aadi," she replied, annoyed.

That was when it hit him. No memory was waiting to be born. He handed the box to her through the narrow crack. "It belonged to mom, and she wanted you to have it."

The door shut faster than the time it took Aadi to turn around.

Panting from the uphill walk in her golden wedges, Megh finally reached the entrance where a brigade of minions in black suits, complete with plenary indulgences including earpieces and walkie-talkies, surrounded a mare. Rambo arrived and locked his gaze with the mare's. Feeling uncomfortable under his impregnable gaze, the skittish mare shuffled her hind legs.

"Cancel it!" Rambo hollered.

An anxious aide of the Tekchand replied, "All arrangements have been made, we cannot cancel it now!"

"Just look at her. She could have mange, lice, or some other skin condition! I can't take that chance. I had specifically stated that the mare needed to be sterilised!" Rambo was beside himself.

"But Memsahib took a bath," the *ghodiwala* stated in protest. "She is my special one. I gave her a bath with Pears soap, sir, never used it on my body also!"

"I am not convinced. She looks highly contaminated!" Rambo continued, more shaken than before. "It is impossible for me to take on this life-threatening journey. Please tell Avanti that the baraat is coming by car, and we will be waiting for her down in the lobby in ten minutes."

Shortly after that announcement, Megh witnessed a tightly-packed Rambo seated between sentries in the backseat of a Rolls Royce as it tailgated the groom-less mare towards the exit of the hotel.

As they disappeared, Megh rushed to the hotel grounds and was greeted by a crew of hostesses, all immaculately draped in tussar silk uniform sarees, welcoming the guests with folded hands. Towards the end of the long line was Eliza.

At the bar, Megh was on her first whiskey when the baraat that had exited from one gate of the hotel arrived through the other. Wthin minutes, the exquisite *mandap* with its intricately decorated flowers became invisible under the weight of its new occupants.

A sudden hush fell all over the place as Avanti made an appearance. Standing at 5'10", donning a stone-worked lehenga that weighed as much as she did, she looked every inch the picture-perfect bride.

Aadi joined Megh at the bar and finished his peg of whiskey in one swig.

"Did you give the necklace to her?"

"Yes."

"Is she wearing it?"

"No idea," he answered, curtly.

Megh realised that he was not in a mood to talk. They stayed at the bar, watching the wedding theatrics unfold till it was time to assume their roles in the act. As proxy parents, they had to 'give away' Avanti, in the *kanyadaan* ceremony. With the havankundli substituted with an electric fire, the *pheras* were a quicker 2.0 version of the original. Aadi ran back to the bar, his presence on stage as short-lived as a New Year's resolution, while Megh lingered on to mingle.

The guest list was select and enviable. There was a roar, announcing the arrival of a star who presided higher than the others in the food chain. It was Subu. He wished the newlyweds, pulled out a gift from his pocket and bent over Avanti to clasp it around her neck.

It was a necklace – a Cartier choker.

It was eleven p.m. The guests had started to dwindle. Eliza felt a deep sense of satisfaction when she learned from her sources that the media conglomerate was planning on suing the Tekchands as the wedding pictures had leaked to the public.

She approached the couple with a big smile. "Here, you can have your phones," she said, handing them over. "Avanti, that one inspector has been trying to reach you. He called many times actually."

"Now what do the police want today!" Sethji scowled. "Police are harassing the public more than goons nowadays, not letting a wedding take place in peace."

Avanti took her phone and dialled the missed caller. "This is Avanti Wadhwa Tekchand on the line. I believe you have been looking for me?"

Chapter 42
The Arrest

Mumbai, 7th July 2016

Reclining in her chair with her legs lounging on the table in her cabin, Urvashi made a phone call. "Hello, Baba, are you sleeping?"

"No, I have been waiting for your call. How did it go?" he asked, his voice laced with anticipation.

"It was perfect. Thank god, I intercepted Hasan's call to Shreyas, and then based on your suggestion, I approached the magistrate to re-open the case. I got her arrest warrant. It wasn't easy, but I got it done. You are a mastermind! He would be taking all the credit had he not been suspended. We will arrest her today. I have also tipped the press so they will be there when it happens."

"Excellent! Excellent, that too just after the wedding which was attended by the movers and shakers that control Mumbai!" He was jubilant. "That Hasan attacking you was the best thing to have happened to your career. All you must do now is keep the media stories alive. Keep her entangled in something or the other. You are going to become the next Kiran Bedi, but Bittu, remember…"

It was the first time in so many years that her baba had called her Bittu.

She replied softly, "Yes, Baba."

"Be careful, don't make any mistakes. Though suspended, Hasan is not the type to give up on a case."

Chapter 43
The Sardar Police Station

Mumbai, 7th July 2016

A sole bulb hung outside. It was naked, stripped of its respect, much like the inmates who were inside the cell.

The police had arrested her. The gears of time had come to a complete halt. Megh remembered what Heidegger had said and let out a small laugh. *Boredom is the awareness of time passing*. She was aware of time passing, but was she bored in a police cell? She looked around. The police station was buzzing with excitement.

The thoughts kept coming. She was surprised that her mind kept returning to Surya. In so many days, she had not let herself think about him. Yet, today, it was as if she was in a movie that was playing on a loop. In the film, she was with Chana, MJ, Ashok, Mishal, and other SGI employees on the terrace with a laughing Surya. He was facing them and walking backwards towards the ledge. They all stood silently as he fell off, but nobody saved him, they didn't even bother trying. No outstretched hands, no screams, no tears, nothing. Just an eerie silence. Instinctively, she touched her face, it was still dry as a drought.

She could see Aadi waiting outside. His face had added an unwanted jowl since last night. He looked defeated.

They had already taken her blood and urine samples. After a while, an officer came in for questioning. She tried hard to focus on the questions.

How long have you known Surya?

Did you have a sexual relationship with him?
Did you know him before you started working at SGI?

There was more chaos; she realised someone had come in, she recognised the voice.

It was Hasan. She wondered what he was doing here. She had learned that he was no longer in charge of the case.

A favour was asked, a favour returned. He got permission to enter the cell. Aadi was allowed to join as well.

Hasan didn't look too happy. The other junior inspector was there with him too.

"Officer, I don't even know why I have been arrested."

"Oh, don't pretend to be so naïve. You have lied, and that's why you are here. Bakr Eid has come early for Urvashi; she is going to feast on you for a long time. You are her ticket to fame," he said with his jaw clenched. "You met Surya, a week before he died, and you didn't disclose that."

Megh's heart sank.

"I got nervous; my intention was not to hide. I mean, if I wanted to hide, would I tell Avanti?" her voice was quivering.

"You went to meet Surya?" Aadi said slowly.

"Hear me out please," she pleaded. "Avanti was complaining to me that she had too much on her hands and going personally to invite her guests was becoming a burden. She told me she had a coffee date fixed with Surya, but had to cancel last minute. I told her I would go instead and give the invite to Surya, and she agreed."

"But you hid that from the police," Hasan pointed out.

"I told you I was scared."

"And did Surya know you were coming instead of Avanti?"

Megh lowered her eyes. "He would never have agreed to meet me. I only wanted to clear the air between us. After the whole scandal, we both had said a lot of bitter things to each other. He would be attending Avanti's wedding, and I wanted both of us to be comfortable. I had no other intention; please believe me," she pleaded.

"How was the meeting?"

"It was fine," she said, forcing herself to calm down, "we sat for about thirty minutes, had coffee and then left."

"You didn't feel it important to tell me?" Aadi added quietly, controlling his anger.

"There was really nothing to tell," she said.

There was a wave of furore announcing another arrival. This time it was Rambo. "Hello, Megh," he said calmly.

"What are *you* doing here?" Megh enquired.

"I came to tell you that you have been fired," he stated matter-of-factly. "Sethji wanted me to inform you over email, but I wanted to deliver the news in person. We're technically family, after all. I also wanted to let you know that I truly enjoyed working with you, and I am sorry."

"Don't be. I understand, but I have one favour to ask you."

"What's that?"

"I have worked very hard on the Divine Cocoa Project," Megh said. "This program has the potential to reach many farmers in India. Please don't stop it now."

He nodded before hurrying off.

Hunched against a corner in the cell without touching any food or water, it was a couple of hours before Aadi returned with her bail.

She squinted as they stepped out of the police station.

A flower seller offered her a *gajra* made from jasmine from her woven basket, "Take one, didi. It will look very good in your hair. Your husband will love you more." She giggled.

Megh bought five pieces from her and tossed it in the garbage bin on her way to the car.

Chapter 44
Rambo

Mumbai, 7th July 2016

His visit to the police station and the battle of the horns between his driver and the other drivers was giving Rambo a headache. Google Maps on his phone was a flaring red, anticipating another hour before he reached his destination. He had scheduled a meeting with Sethji to discuss the Divine Cocoa Project with him one more time. He had to get rid of the headache. He asked his driver to pull up at a nearby medical store.

"A bottle of mineral water and a packet of Panadol, please," he said, his hands deep inside his pockets, clenching the mini wipes packet. He felt a pair of eyes bore into him. It was a young boy. His one hand was locked under the crook of his mother's hand, and in the other, he was holding a chocolate. The mother was getting the *hisab* done for her list.

"I want the chocolate," the kid said, suddenly turning his attention to her.

"No, I said, chocolates are bad for you. You had one yesterday – too much sugar. Mummy is a doctor, and she doesn't want your teeth rotting from all that sugar," she stated. Rambo wondered why she had chosen this moment to divulge the details of her profession to her son and everyone else around.

"Madam, this one is made out of Stevia. It's a really good sugar substitute," the chemist said.

157

"How much is it for?" the mother asked.

"Only forty-seven rupees," he replied.

"Madam, if I may, I have a question for you." Rambo said, shocked at himself for initiating a conversation with a stranger. "If a chocolate cost twenty percent more, would you buy it?"

The mother looked at him, startled, "Of course not! Why would I pay so much more?"

"So that the additional money could go towards the empowerment of the farmers. So that perhaps their children too can get access to education and eat a chocolate sometimes," Rambo stated.

"I make so many donations already. I can't be giving out my hard-earned money to solve all the world's problems."

Before Rambo got a chance to explain any further, the chemist pointed to a troupe of hijras headed their way, "Oh no, here they come again! Such a menace."

"Amma, Amma," the leader of the hijras said, aiming for the mother, their immediate target.

"Give us some money so we can bless your prince, the ruler of your world!"

The mother didn't offer any reply or money.

"Amma, if you don't pay, we will curse him!" they threatened.

The mother pulled her son towards her quickly. The little boy was afraid. It was his first encounter with the hijra community – a community that had been degraded and dehumanized so much that even today, they found it hard to be a part of society without facing discrimination. Unable to find gainful employment elsewhere, they continued to sing and dance at births and weddings to sustain themselves.

Not getting the desired reaction, they decided to up their verbal ante with a sexual chip. Mistaking Rambo to be the boy's father, they started clapping and making obscene gestures at him.

"No, no, no, no," Rambo protested, but his aggressive refusal only added to their vehemence. They mischievously threatened to lift their petticoats and offer him some tips for increasing his libido. Quickly grabbing his merchandise, Rambo darted towards his car. It was only after he was seated and had wiped down his entire body , did he realise that the car hadn't moved at all.

"What happened?" he asked his driver.

"That," the driver pointed to a procession of cows that had decided to pay the neighbourhood a visit. Rambo sighed. After gulping his Panadol with an entire bottle of water, he rolled down his window for some fresh air and witnessed the transaction between the mother and the hijras in its final stages.

The mother handed the leader a hundred-rupee note, and they, in return, bestowed the boy with their blessings and moved on.

Rambo wondered how the opposing ideas of science and superstition could live together in the same head. He was perplexed how a doctor could resist the idea of helping farmers, but had readily loosened the strings of her purse against an invisible curse. Suddenly, he saw the young boy outside his Mercedes.

"What is the name?" the boy demanded.

"Name of what?" Rambo asked, bewildered.

"Of that chocolate for the farmer's children?"

"Divine."

"You make it. I will buy it!" the boy declared. "When I grow up, I will buy Divine Chocolates."

Chapter 45
Hasan

The waiting area in the clinic was full.

Hasan found an empty seat outside the pantry where he could overhear the conversation between the peon and the nurse who were eating their *dabba* for lunch.

"What is his problem? The new case?"

"Who? The one who is chewing like the cow?"

"Yes."

"He thinks something is stuck in his throat."

"So, why doesn't he remove it?"

"Because there is nothing."

"*Baapre*, that also happens?"

"Yes."

"I didn't know about this illness. I only know of Enzaty, Panic, Depress, ADHD, Bulima, Arexa…" he rattled off mental health problems like an Udipi restaurant waiter listing the items on the menu.

Hasan wondered which one, according to the peon, was he on the menu card.

After a long wait, the nurse approached him, "The doctor will see you now," she remarked, and led him to Dr Poonawala's consulting room.

"How are you doing?" Dr Poonawala enquired.

"I am doing just great. This suspension is actually helping me relax."

160

"You look much better."

"I wanted to talk to you about…" just then Hasan got a WhatsApp notification.

"Oh! My day just got much better! Unfortunately, I will have to cancel today's session as I have to get somewhere," Hasan said jubilantly, heading for the door.

"You seem very happy. Did you save someone? Someone got married? Had a baby? Which one?"

"Someone died!" Hasan replied cheerfully before rushing out of the clinic.

Chapter 46
Imperial Towers I

Mumbai, 14th July 2016

...you were never pretty or intelligent, but you were likable. That was your only quality, but I was wrong. You are a despicable human.

Chana was frowning at her laptop. She couldn't believe Megh would send her an email like that. Surely there had drifted apart post the D'sire party incident, but this was downright nasty! The intercom buzzed. It was that new receptionist again. Chana picked up the phone and sighed, "What is it now?"

"You know that officer Hasan? He is here to see Ashok sir."

"So?" Chana growled.

"So should I buzz sir?"

"I am not Ashok's PA; why are you asking me?"

"I read in the papers that officer Hasan had been suspended, so I wasn't sure."

Chana was suddenly attentive. She was not that bird-brained after all. "Yes, just connect him with Ashok sir. As long as he is not entering our offices, we are fine."

Swivelling back towards her laptop, Chana was surprised to see Bhanu leaning over and smiling at her.

"They call me for everything as if I am everyone's secretary," Chana explained, wondering if Bhanu had picked up the irritation in her voice.

"It's because you are so reliable," Bhanu said. "I need your assistance as well. Babuj— MJ has sent me here to get

162

a blue file. And I have no idea what he is talking about," she said, throwing her hands up in the air.

"Not a problem. I'm actually grateful for your presence. Since you have started coming to the office, MJ has been bothering me less," Chana replied.

As if to prove her wrong, MJ called her on the intercom and huffed, "I've sent Bhanu to get the blue file. What's taking so long?"

Chana winked at Bhanu and replied, "She will be there in a minute."

"At least he sounds like his good old self now, yelling at everyone," Chana remarked as she handed over the blue file.

Bhanu nodded, "That's true. At one time, we thought we were going to lose him too," Bhanu's eyes started welling up. "But he is a fighter, and his mind is sharp as ever."

Bhanu forced a smile and walked away. She was at the door when Chana called out again. "By the way, I forgot to mention earlier that Dr Chawla, the company doctor, wants a copy of MJ's medical report and prescriptions."

"Sure, I will send it across."

Chana's intercom buzzed again. "You better hurry," Chana mouthed at Bhanu, "it's him again!"

Chana watched Bhanu walk into MJ's cabin and hand him the file. She gently smoothed down his static hair and found his spectacles that were buried under stacks of papers.

What a contrast between the brother and sister, Chana thought to herself. She had never seen Ashok do anything so endearing for his father.

Her eyes darted back to Megh's email. Rereading it riled her up even more, and she called her mother in Italy. "I shouldn't have taken your advice! Send her a nice email, you said. Look what she wrote back! That bitch!"

Chapter 47
Fathers

Mumbai, 14th July 2016

Hasan was collecting his coffee from the self-service counter when he saw Ashok walk through the doors of the café. He marched towards Hasan.

"What do you want? What was the meaning of leaving that ridiculous message that if I love my son, and want to find out who the murderer is, I must meet you immediately. He was not murdered! It was an accident," Ashok seethed.

"I am glad you came. At least it shows you have some balls. Please take a seat," Hasan said cordially.

"What is it that you wanted to tell me?"

"What was your relationship with Ali?"

"What do you mean?" Ashok replied stiffly.

"Why did you hire him?"

Ashok remained quiet.

"Look, Megh told me everything. I know that you admitted to colluding with Ali to use ADR in D'sire. I have also seen the CCTV footage of you meddling with Ali's computer, but I need to understand that if you were responsible, then how come Toni's name came up in the report?"

"I don't know how his name got there," Ashok mumbled.

"What is the name of the vendor that supplied the ADR? How much did you order?"

"I don't know," Ashok fumbled, staring at his hands. "It was all Ali's decision."

"But you signed and paid for it. You must know the amount. How much?"

Ashok remained silent.

"You don't know because you have no clue. This is the story you told Surya when he confronted you about Ali. You said yes, as that let you cover up the real reason that led you to delete everything from Ali's computer. You had nothing to do with ADR," Hasan said with finality. "Ali was blackmailing you for something else and you went to his office to delete that evidence, didn't you?"

Ashok continued to stare at his hands.

"I know you transferred fifty lakhs to Ali's account in Lagos. Now, why was he blackmailing you? What's your dirty secret?" Hasan asked quietly.

"I was introduced to Ali by someone who makes these connections… between men," Ashok began. "Ali and I, we had an affair. He really understood me. Then one day, he said that he was looking for a job. He had decent experience in manufacturing in food companies, and I saw this as the perfect opportunity to have him close to me at work. We were recruiting anyway. So I offered him the job, and he took it. But as soon as he started working here, he turned cold towards me. I wanted to fire him, but I could not, as he was a part of the D'sire project that was doing so well."

"Then right after the D'sire party, he sent me a text blackmailing me with some pictures. He threatened to leak the pictures to my father, and the tabloids as well. I paid him the ransom, and he told me where I could find the evidence."

"Surya knew about this?"

"No."

"And MJ?"

"Once, when I was in my twenties, Babuji had caught me with a boy. He had tortured me for days until I swore and told him that I would never do it again. That's also why he got me married off so early. He can't find out about this. He will be devastated. Please, you have to promise me," Ashok pleaded.

"So when Surya asked you if you were involved in the ADR fiasco, you just took the blame?"

"Yes."

"And Surya didn't question how Toni's name got on the report?"

"I told him I tampered with the report and put Toni's name there. I told him it was me who bought the ADR and sanctioned its use so that his chocolate would be successful."

"You took the blame for your brother-in-law's actions and his eventual death on your hands to save your secret?" Hasan asked, shocked by the revelation.

"I didn't kill Toni. I, in fact, took the blame for what Toni had done. I am the one who came out looking like the loser in front of my son! My son died thinking I was a murderer and a cheat!" Ashok rubbed his temples in defeat.

"This is not making any sense. I realised that Ali was blackmailing you, and I thought that you told Surya about it, and Surya got him killed."

"Wait! What? Ali is dead?" Ashok looked up, shocked.

"Yes, Ali is dead."

"How is that possible?"

"A car ran over him in Lagos. It was made to look like an accident. I just found out. Did someone know about your affair?"

"Nobody," Ashok responded meekly. "As I said, after Ali joined SGI, he was not interested in me."

"What are you doing here?"

Hasan heard Urvashi before he saw her. "I think I am allowed to have coffee wherever I want," pointing to Ashok, he continued. "And he also came in to get a cuppa. The gentleman that he is, when he saw me, he stopped by to say hello, right Ashok sahib?"

"Yes, I was just going to get my coffee."

"Goodbye," Hasan said. "I was leaving anyway," he added and walked out.

Hasan could feel Urvashi's gaze bore through his skull as he walked onto the street.

Hasan's mind was still reeling from Ashok's revelations when he heard someone call out to him. It was Shreyas. He turned around and saw both Shreyas and Vilas stride towards him with wide grins. A warm feeling came over Hasan. For a moment, he felt a deep desire to run and hug them, but he stopped suddenly instead. It was as if his legs were protecting his heart from getting vulnerable.

Baffled, Shreyas and Vilas stopped too.

The space between them was too close for a handshake, but too far for a hug.

"Sir," said Shreyas, his face suddenly dark, the smile melting into a stricken expression.

"Yes, Shreyas."

"I am sorry, sir. I had orders not to share the details of Avanti's call with you. I also tried to tell the commissioner multiple times about Sharda ma'am's statement, but ..." he said, letting his arms fall listlessly.

"Don't worry about it," Hasan smiled reassuringly. "So, Vilas, how are you doing?"

"First class, sir!" Vilas grinned.

"Sir, I think you must go now. Urvashi ma'am will come out any moment," Shreyas cautioned.

Hasan nodded and turned towards the street, but an emotion tugged at his heart. It was a feeling he had never experienced before, and just as suddenly, he engulfed Vilas in a bear hug.

He embraced Shreyas next, but his show of affection was unreciprocated. He noticed that Shreyas' face was battered with worry.

"What's wrong?"

"I just got a message," he said, holding his phone in his hand for proof. "My wife Savita fell from a chair. She was cleaning a cupboard. She is pregnant. They have taken her to Khambatta Hospital!"

Without uttering a word, both Vilas and Hasan mobilised into action. They almost dragged the dazed Shreyas and forced him into the jeep. Vilas stabbed the key in the ignition, and the jeep took off at an alarming speed.

Hasan was inflicted by the same pain that agonized Shreyas. He wanted to say something to console him, but the words just wouldn't come out of his mouth.

This wave of concern for another person was new to him. He remembered Dr Poonawala's words: *You need to build empathy – brick by brick – to feel human again.* He was finally making a breakthrough.

They sped through a signal. Hasan caught sight of a young girl begging on the street; she was balancing her sibling on her slender hips. The kid locked his arms around her with a certain sense of entitlement that only love can sanction. Suddenly he could see children everywhere: On the bike riding next to their vehicle, a child was sandwiched tightly between his parents; a couple with their children in a taxi, a mother holding her daughter's hand as they crossed the road.

"Do you know anything about children?" Hasan asked Vilas as they sped through a signal.

"I should, I have two," Vilas answered.

"You do?" Hasan was surprised. He stared at Vilas's earnest face as if this bit of information was written somewhere on it and he had missed reading it.

"Aren't they a burden, on your salary?"

"Yes, sir. A big burden."

"Then?"

"Sir, to have a burden is a privilege only a few get to experience in their life," Vilas responded, giving Shreyas a reassuring half-smile.

The jeep cramped itself through the narrow gate of the hospital, and immediately Shreyas' mother appeared at his window wearing a big smile.

"You have become a father of a baby girl," she shouted in joy, taking both his hands in hers. "Both Savita and the baby are doing fine."

Relief washed over Shreyas' face. The tears started flowing freely as he hugged everyone and ran to visit his wife.

Hasan and Vilas waited patiently outside the double-sharing room where Savita was recuperating. Finally, Shreyas emerged along with his brother, Shivu.

"I am going to take you to show you the baby," dictated Shivu with authority, "but everyone must follow the rules. The baby has come soon and is tiny, so she is still in NICU."

"Yes sir!" Hasan said, slapping him with a salute that thrilled the young man.

Peering through the glass of the NICU, Shivu pointed her out to them. Hasan watched with amazement as her body, the size of his palm, was attached to many tubes, but her tiny heart was beating fiercely.

"Her head is so big, like ET," he said, intrigued.

"What did you just call my daughter?" Shreyas said, laughing loudly.

"So, what have you decided to name her?" Shreyas' mother asked.

"I am going to pick a cricketer's name!"

"Bhaiya, we can't give her a boy's name," Shivu reasoned.

"I know," he smiled, "I was going to suggest Mithali, after the captain of the Indian women's cricket team."

"Super idea! Let me tell bhabhi," Shivu said, running back into the room.

"Sir, I have no words." Shreyas' eyes welled up again. "You stayed here with me on my life's most important day. I am indebted to you forever. My daughter is blessed to have your hand over her head all her life."

"I haven't done anything, and you can't be sure that I will be around for your daughter. What if I travel? Leave the city?"

"You won't leave the city!" Shreyas shook his head with assurance.

"Why not?"

"Your old father lives here alone. You can't leave him."

"And what about your mother?" Shreyas' mother interjected. "Is she dead?"

"No, not dead," Hasan replied softly.

"Keep quiet, Aai! You can't ask such questions," Shreyas reprimanded his mother.

"Thank god, she is alive," she said, folding her hands.

Shreyas shook his head at his mother and suddenly said, "Mithali doesn't mind if you travel, go for a short holiday. I think you should go to Kerala."

"Good idea!" seconded Vilas. "You should go to Kerala and drink coconut water all day. You are like a coconut only, sir. Hard from the outside and soft on the inside."

"I agree I need a break. But I think I will go to Bengaluru, not Kerala."

Chapter 48
D'Souza

Bengaluru, 17th July 2016

Hasan stepped out of the airport with his cabin luggage in tow and glanced at his watch. His face broke out into a smile. D'Souza was late – as usual. The familiarity comforted him. A pathological latecomer in college, D'Souza's stories for being late were notorious. His mastery of the art was so great that if, on a rare occasion, D'Souza arrived on time, his friends chastised him for the great outlandish lie they were left bereft of.

After Salma and Farhan's affair, Hasan had cut ties with his entire college squad, including D'Souza. They had all reached out to him, some expressing sympathy, others to console him, and a few, offering their imagination to pepper the truth. But he had excised those years as if they were a tumour.

Being suspended the first time had added to the fragility of his mind and provided him with the time to continually harbour suspicions against everyone. Somehow this suspension felt different. Watching the pride with which Shreyas and Vilas carried the burden of their relationships had made Hasan yearn for his own. Hesitantly, he had called D'Souza, and the warmth of his *'Chutia, kahan hain tu?'* had melted away his vacillation.

"Hasan!"

As he turned around, he was immediately engulfed in a bear hug by a much heavier D'Souza.

"*Saale*, you are still late!" Hasan complained.

"You won't believe what happened. I left earlier than usual to pick you up, but on the way, I stopped at MTR restaurant to get a dosa packed. I had just collected the parcel from the restaurant when a pack of street dogs attacked me, snatched the packet, and ran. I am sure a gang of beggars are training these dogs to go after MTR's parcels. The dogs came back to take the packed sambar and chutney from my other hand as well! I had to chase them. I am police, after all."

Hasan buckled down with laughter.

"How come you decided to come to Bengaluru all of a sudden? It can't be just to meet me. Does it have something to do with the Surya Jain case?"

"That," Hasan admitted, "amongst other things. Our prime suspect, Megh, lived a good part of her life here in Bengaluru before moving to Mumbai; her guardian still lives here."

"I read in the papers that you were the first to suggest that Megh had something to do with Surya Jain's death, and that Urvashi just hogged all the credit. But the truth will come out. We will tell the world it was you."

"That Urvashi is really on Megh's heels now and will use her for her promotion. I have to get to the truth."

"So now you think Megh might not be the culprit?" D'Souza questioned.

"I am not so sure," Hasan admitted. "The last two years, I had a very blinkered view of everything," he continued as they loaded his bag into the boot. "But I want to make sure that if Megh is not the culprit, then I am not the one who sent her to her death sentence. For once, I want to see everything for what it really is."

The two hours in the traffic were spent well catching up on old stories and new developments. Hasan learned that D'Souza lived with his wife Genelia, his six-year-old son, and an ageing mother in a 2BHK flat in Sarjapur. He also learned about Salma and Farhan's break up. That piece of information was carefully sandwiched between other occurrences and was served to him as a side dish.

At home, Genelia served him dosa with goan prawn curry for dinner. The futon in their living room had been converted into a bed for him. After changing into his pyjamas, Hasan was ready to pass out when he found the grandmother-grandson duo seated on his makeshift bed watching a comedy show, and shelling peas. Together, they laughed loudly at the jokes and the crude mimicry. Meanwhile in the kitchen, the cooker hooted and whistled incessantly. "Everyone takes a tiffin in the morning, so we prefer to do the preparations in the night," the grandmother said apologetically. Life at the D'Souza's was a far cry from what Hasan was used to. Here it was living casually and laughing aimlessly. To Hasan's mind, this din of everyday life was like a cold cloth on his feverish thoughts. He didn't realise when seated next to them, he drifted off into a deep sleep.

The next morning, over yet another round of dosas, but this time with its usual companions of sambhar and chutney, D'Souza began whining, "Saale, I took the day off for you. I thought I would get to hang out with you, take you to Rocket, but…"

"Rocket?"

"Yeah, it's a famous pub here, it has the best deals on food and booze. But you are making me work!" he complained.

"Come on man, you shouldn't be eating and drinking anymore, or you will burst," Hasan chided him light-heartedly.

"You sound just like Genelia!" D'Souza grumbled. "So tell me, where are we going first?"

Hasan pulled out his phone and showed him the address.

"You sure Megh's guardian lives there?" he frowned.

"Why?"

"That's a very old rundown area. I thought this Megh was rich. By the way, you wanted me to track down Ali Asger. I found out that he went to St Joseph's School. Only his mother's name is on file, Jean, no father's name. All fees were paid via cheques."

"Maybe Megh and Ali went to the same school?" Hasan sounded off excitedly.

"Already thought of that," D'Souza said and handed him a brown envelope. "It contains a list of all the students in school with him. This has been quite a task as there were no computers then; my boys compiled the list manually," he added proudly.

Hasan opened it and perused the list. "There is a Megha Narain and Meghana Gauda, but no Megh Madan, which is her maiden name," he said pouring over it. "I didn't realise there would be so many variations of Megh, that it was such a common Kannadiga name."

"Bengaluru is a very metropolitan city, just like Mumbai," D'Souza protested loudly. "We have people from everywhere and names from everywhere! We are the Silicon Valley of India."

"Okay, okay!" Hasan laughed. "By the way, I had sent you the bank details where Ashok had transferred the funds? Were you able to find out anything?"

"That money has not been withdrawn," D'Souza stated.

"Not been withdrawn?"

"Maybe he died before that."

"Nope, he died almost one week after the transfer."

"That's strange, isn't it?" D'souza pondered. "All that trouble to get the money, and when the money comes, you don't withdraw it."

"Unless blackmail was never the real motive," Hasan thought out loud.

"What do you mean?"

"Ali had to show that he was blackmailing Ashok for the money, but maybe there was another motive."

"Like what?"

"I hope we find out soon."

The address took them to an old building. They rang the doorbell of an apartment on the ground floor.

"Priya Madan?" D'Souza asked the woman who opened the door.

"Yes?"

"We are from the police and wanted to ask you a few questions about Megh."

"Megh? Is she alright?" the woman stammered with worry.

"She is fine, but she is the primary accused in a murder case."

"She mentioned something about that boy, Surya's death the last time we spoke, but not that she was the accused. How can she be when she hasn't done anything?" she protested.

"We would like to believe that, but we must admit that she has been hiding a lot of information from us," Hasan forewarned.

"I want to speak with her first," Priya declared.

"Madam, don't do that," Hasan said, quickly sticking his foot between them and the door.

"If she is innocent, then you should be willing to help us out," D'Souza added quickly.

Priya Madan thought for a moment before finally letting them in.

"What do you want to know?" she asked.

"Can you tell us about Megh's childhood... her family? I believe you are not her mother, and you are called PM?" Hasan relayed what he knew.

"Priya Madan," she smiled. "I am her *bua*. Her father's sister. She was born in Los Angeles. Her mother died of cancer when she was six years old. She lost her father ten years later."

"That must have been very traumatic," Hasan stated.

"Yes it was, they had all come here for a holiday, and the kids insisted that they wanted to stay longer, so their father extended their stay, and he went back to resume work. He died in a car accident a week later."

"Kids? Megh has a sibling?" Hasan asked, surprised.

PM looked uneasy for a moment, as if she had let out a big secret.

"Yes, a younger brother; six years younger to her."

"And where is he?"

"San Francisco."

"So you took them both in after their father died?"

"Yes, as their blood relative, I took custody of the kids."

"And your family?"

"I was very young when the kids came into my life, and even though they attended boarding schools in Panchgani, they became my life. No one wants to marry someone with two kids."

"Did Megh ever mention Surya or Ali to you? Ali Asger, is originally from Nigeria, but apparently has connections with Bengaluru as well."

"No, she didn't officer, I am getting late. I have to go somewhere actually. "

"Okay. Thank you for all your help."

As they headed for the door, Hasan was distracted by a picture that hung over a lace-covered landline phone. A much younger, but unmistakable Megh was sharing a smile with a good-looking middle-aged man who seemed to be her father. The resemblance was striking. His arm was engulfed around the neck of a young boy. The sister, a younger Priya, was smiling lovingly at her brother.

"That's a lovely photo," Hasan told Priya.

"Yeah, this one was taken in Mysore," she said, nostalgically.

As soon as the police left and the door closed, PM jabbed her phone.

"You were right, he came here today!" Priya exclaimed into the phone. "But how did you know that he was going to come all the way to Bengaluru?"

"I didn't know for sure," Aadi admitted, "but I have seen some zealous police officers in my profession. Hasan belongs to that category. I figured that that would be his next logical step – to investigate Megh's childhood."

"Well…"

"What's wrong?" Aadi's voice was heavy with concern.

"I mentioned Sid. It was a mistake."

Chapter 49
Chana

Mumbai, 18th July 2016

The building was an old construction with no elevator. Despite each stair being steep, Chana could usually vault up in her heels, but today, she dragged her feet over the footprints of yesteryears. Megh's snarky email had not let her sleep well for the last couple of days. Most of the residents of the building had moved out as the water pipe had broken down. The repair work should have taken two days, but today was day six and there was still no sign of water in the taps. Unlike the others, Chana was holding up just fine. *Indians fussed too much about cooking food at home, and for that, they consumed too much water,* she thought to herself. Living alone, she hardly cooked, and moving elsewhere temporarily was such a nuisance.

Of course, she needed water for her bathroom rituals, but she used the next door Gymkhana's facilities for that.

With her shoes kicked off, and her clothes flung on the floor, Chana floated around naked in her 1BHK, heating the leftovers in the microwave, and setting her table for one. She awaited the arrival of Old Monk, the antidote to her sombre thoughts, from her local alcohol delivery shop. A WhatsApp ping assured her that her two bottles were on their way.

The doorbell rang. Tying a towel around her body like a sarong, Chana waded towards the door, picking up a twenty-rupee note from her wallet to tip the delivery boy.

She opened the door.

Chapter 50
Ammi

"Why are we going to Devara Jeevanahalli?" D'Souza asked.

"I have to meet someone."

"In a slum in Bengaluru?"

"Yes."

"Who?"

"Someone."

D'Souza didn't like being kept in the dark. But something told him to hold off on the persistent questioning.

"*Chal*, let's go to Rocket this evening. You and me, for old times' sake?" Hasan suggested, distracting him.

A smile slowly spread across D'Souza's face.

Hasan had no recollection of his mother. Only pieces reconstructed from old pictures. His memory failed him for the most part, except for one recollection of a skinny, placid-natured, saree-clad woman gliding silently in and out of the dining room, putting freshly made rotis on his plate. It was the only solid memory he had of her.

He knocked on a door that was the colour of unburnished silver, as if defiled from years of water damage. As it opened, the scent of Cuticura talcum powder wafted towards him. He realised that he had retained that particular smell. After all these years, his Ammi was in front of him.

179

"As-Salaam-Alaikum, Ammijaan," Hasan's voice wobbled, tears silently drenching his face.

"Wa-Alaikum-Salaam, Wa-Alaikum-Salaam. Who do you want to meet?" she shouted, as if hard of hearing.

"It's me Hasan, your son."

"Who?" she asked again.

"Hasan."

Suddenly her humped back straightened. She reached out and placed her hands on his forearm.

They were cold and bony, but her grip was surprisingly strong for her fragile body.

"Hasan?" she whispered to reconfirm.

Hasan simply nodded.

"Oh my son, why have you come here?"

"Why did you abandon me?" he blurted out like a child, unable to hold his anger.

"Oh, my son, my son…" she started touching his face. "Come in!" she said in a hushed voice, suddenly aware that they were exposed to a hundred other houses in the shanty.

Hasan hunched down under the low ceiling and sat on the chipped red-tiled floor, waiting for her to talk.

It took her a long while before she finally spoke. Tears were silently rolling down her face as she rummaged the memories she had shunted aside.

"I came from a poor family, from a small village, and I was married off to your father as he was well to do, much richer than my family. I moved with him to Mumbai. Then you came along. Your father worked from morning to night. I was lonely. I didn't know anyone. Then I met him. He was a plumber. I fell in love with him," she admitted.

"Your father found out. The whole colony did," she laughed. "He shouted at everyone in the colony, told them to keep quiet, and asked me if I wanted to stay or go. I said I wanted to go. He asked me if I wanted to take you or leave you. Yes, he asked me. But I knew that your Abu loved you more than anyone else in the world. My new husband wouldn't love you like your Abu. I am sorry, but I did what I thought was right for you. And today after so many years," she ran her hand on the outlines of his face, "you came looking for me. Will you ever forgive me?"

"You didn't even check how I was doing," Hasan said in a dazed voice. *His Abu had never told him that his mother didn't want him. In fact, he always made him feel that he was very loved by his mother.*

"How was I to check, who could I ask?" she said innocently. She sighed before she asked, "How did you find me?"

"I am a police officer, Ammi. I find people; that's my job."

"You are a police officer?" Her eyes widened in surprise. "Yes, I remember. You always wanted to be in the police!" Suddenly remembering something, she got up. "*Arrey*, I haven't offered you anything, there isn't much food…" she said, dragging herself to the corner of the small room that housed a single stove.

She stopped midway, "I hope you are not looking to stay here; there is hardly any place," she said, waving her hand across the small room.

"I am not staying," he replied quietly.

"You must leave soon. My son, my other son. He is at work now, but he will be coming home shortly. He gets angry very quickly."

"I am going," Hasan said, realising that their worlds were very different. His frail and innocent mother lived another life now, unaware of the consequences that her elopement had set in motion in a little boy in Mumbai.

On his way out, he dug his hand into his pocket and slipped a bundle of notes to her.

"No need to tell anyone."

She nodded, patting his hand in gratitude.

Back in the car, they rode silently for a while. D'Souza tried to make small talk, but didn't get any response.

After a while, D'Souza probed again, "Are you okay?"

"We live in these imagined realities of love and service, but at the core of it all, we are all selfish bastards living for ourselves. All along, I imagined that my mother had tried to contact me, but couldn't. I was so wrong. What a foolish man I have been to hope that she would remember me. She remembers nothing. Nothing! I never wanted to be a policeman!"

Chapter 51
The Rocket

Bengaluru, 18th July 2016

They were escorted to the bar of the space shuttle inspired pub The Rocket. Hands outstretched, D'Souza beamed with the pride of a magician who had just conjured the missing damsel, expecting an applause from his solo audience.

Hasan, rooted to the ground, eyed the interiors of the restaurant with pronounced skepticism. He suspected that the whole purpose of a creation that involved throbbing walls painted in garish kabuki colours and pulsating lights was to partially blind Bengaluru. Grabbing their vodkas, they managed to flop themselves in an astronaut-shaped pod, when D'Souza made another incredulous recommendation.

"Let's do Karaoke! They have everything. Hindi, English, Kannada, even Korean songs!"

Hasan agreed, surprising D'Souza and himself. He let D'Souza make the choices and for the duets, he even sang the female portion of the song!

Four jarring renditions later, after re-living the fortitude of youth with the fragility of middle age, they were in a cab, leafing through college memories, when Hasan's cell phone rang.

It was Shreyas.

"Shreyas, my friend!"

"Sir? Are you drunk, sir?"

"Me? Not at all! Tell me?"

"Sir, you need to come back," his tone was serious.

"Why?"

"Chana has been murdered."

"Wh – whhaat?"

Shreyas detected a slight slur.

"Yes, sir," he spoke slowly. "Megh is one of the suspects. They found a nasty email that she had sent to Chana, last week, really nasty." He repeated for emphasis. "Her husband has managed to get her bail. She is in deep trouble, sir."

"Shreyas, why are you telling me all this? I am off the case."

"That's because Megh wants to talk and says she will only speak with you. You have been put in charge of the case again. Commissioner sir said something like you have a good nose for such things or something like that."

"And what about Urvashi?"

"Urvashi madam has been moved to another case," he said.

Chapter 52
Confessions

With the warmth of D'Souza's bear hug deeply entrenched in his heart, Hasan quickly brought himself up to speed on the case on his way back to Mumbai.

The news was everywhere. Chana's murder had garnered a lot of attention. The deplorable, ethically-corrupt media was having a feast: The reportage ranged from *'After the CEO, the PA was next to go'* to *'Kisne chheeni Chana ki saansein?'* (*Who stole Chana's life?*) The anchors had various experts speculating another murder at SGI. This conjecture was enough to force the State to reopen the SJ death case. And just as suddenly, Hasan was being touted as a hero for having been the first to suspect a more in-depth story.

But even Hasan had to admit that this was completely unexpected. A brutal murder. Chana had been gagged to death. She lived in one of the old buildings with no security, and with the building having water issues, many people had moved out temporarily. No one had reported anything unusual. The police were trying to gather CCTV footage from nearby stores. It was evident that the motive was not money, as there was nothing taken from her apartment.

Hasan read the copy of the email Megh had sent to her:

…You were never pretty or intelligent, but you were likeable. That was your only quality, but I was wrong. You are a despicable human.

Deep down, he hoped that Megh hadn't written it.

185

Why do you care so much about her? D'Souza had asked him that question in Bengaluru. It had startled him, because until that point, he hadn't realized that he did care.

"Because she is misunderstood, like me," Hasan had replied honestly.

Hasan was shocked to see Megh. She had lost considerable weight since he had last seen her. Her face looked gaunt and her clothes hung loosely over her body. Aadi too had aged. The lines around his mouth had suddenly become more visible.

"You said you wanted to talk to me," Hasan said, looking at Megh.

"Yes," Megh responded. "But I have a request. I want to speak with you alone."

Hasan took in a deep breath and glanced at Shreyas as he contemplated her request.

"I am leaving," Shreyas said dutifully, jumping out of his chair.

"I didn't mean you," Megh clarified, and her gaze fell upon Aadi.

Aadi looked at her in disbelief. Without uttering a word, he left.

Hasan stared at Megh. Her eyes were brimming with tears. He could see the decision had tormented her.

"I didn't kill Chana," she said, the sobs escaping her lips.

Hasan had seen many attractive women cry. There was a strange ethereal beauty in grief, making the griever appear alluring and even virtuous, but tears on Megh looked like a violation. He wanted them to stop.

"Did you send her that email?" he asked in a quiet voice, hoping she would say no.

"Yes," she replied.

"Why?"

She took a sharp breath, "I learned recently that Aadi was having an affair – with Chana. She was sending him erotic messages, and at the same time, she was texting me, pretending to revive our dead friendship. I couldn't handle the hypocrisy, so I told her off."

"Did you confront her or Aadi?"

"No! I wanted to see when Aadi would tell me, or if he would tell me at all."

"This is ridiculous. So you are working on an assumption. Maybe Chana was not having an affair with your husband?"

"When I heard about Chana's death, I confronted Aadi, and he confessed."

"Do you have proof of the affair?"

"I mirrored his WhatsApp," she stated simply. "I could read all his messages in real time."

She handed over her phone to him.

"You should have been a detective with your sleuthing skills," he said.

"Aadi should thank me for these sleuthing skills. Isn't that ironic?" She laughed. "His affair was bound to get him into trouble, but now the messages clearly show that they were not together on the night that Chana died. His wife's spying will protect him."

"What did he say about his affair?"

"What can he say?" she shook her head. "That I had changed over the years, that I didn't care about him, that I was a gold digger who married him for his money, all the usual things a man pins on a woman for his own failings."

Hasan felt an arrow of guilt pierce his heart. *He* had told a man who was having an extra marital affair that his wife was a gold digger.

"He doesn't seem that type," Hasan said. "He seems really progressive and supportive."

Megh gathered her thoughts before she spoke. "Aadi is an indulgent husband," she said. "He had an affluent childhood, whereas I had to work very hard to acquire my place in this world.

"To do that takes a lot of discipline. Initially, he liked all that, my commitment and my discipline.

"He was intrigued by my chutzpah. I was different from the other high society girls who were a part of his circle. But those very qualities were not appealing anymore, as soon as I became his wife. He liked the *idea* that I was working, but I was not to carry any residue back home. I was to park my problems in the office, whereas he could brood if things were not right. If I complained, then the standard response was *'Why don't you quit? It's not like we need the money.'* Sometimes, it's not about the money, it's about your identity."

Shreyas could see that she was baring her soul.

"He probably would have been happier with a wife who would put his needs over everything else and would *still* have an interest or a job, but which was low on her priority list. But building a career, officer, takes sacrifices, and I don't think he was ready for that. I haven't changed. I had always wanted a career. It's he who had misunderstood what he wanted in a partner."

Nobody spoke for a while. It dawned on Shreyas that he had a long way to go before he could truly become a progressive husband. Language such as 'allowing her to work' and expecting strokes of praise for that mindset was just as traditionalistic, and probably more damaging.

Hasan was reminded of the evening when she had enlightened him about Ardhanarishvara. She had truly embodied that concept. Images from his life were looming in front of him and making him uncomfortable. He had been far from perfect towards Salma, but he dismissed those thoughts for now.

"Who do you think killed Chana?" Hasan asked.

"I have no idea."

"She had any enemies?"

"Not that I know of."

"Where were you at the time of her death?"

"Rambo had requested me to accompany him to a town hall with the farmers. The Divine Cocoa project is close to my heart, and even though I am fired, I want to do everything I can to see it become a success," she sounded genuine. "You can check with Rambo; he will vouch for me."

"Tell me one thing," Hasan asked her as they neared the end of the investigation. "Why did you ask to speak only to me?"

"Because you know what it feels like to be cheated on." The pain was written all over her face.

Chapter 53
Murders

Mumbai, 20th July 2016

Hasan and Shreyas passed through a door with floor-to-ceiling mirrors that parted to unveil one of Mumbai's best-kept secrets – the penthouse of Island Towers. A wedding gift from Sethji to the couple, the duplex penthouse spanned over 7000 sq. feet on the sixtieth floor of one of Mumbai's skyscrapers. The butler led them to the terrace with a plunge pool where they waited for Rambo by the deck.

Two French bulldogs, one fawn and one white, sauntered in and obliged them with a sniff.

Shreyas recognised the liveried dog nanny who was pushing the white one in a stroller in the lobby.

"He was just downstairs, right? What's his name?" he asked.

"Vanilla," the nanny replied.

"Does he have trouble with his legs?"

"Madam doesn't let him walk on the roads. It is so dirty everywhere. He is only allowed to play in the dog park."

With that, she scooped them off and gently placed them in the pool where they waddled on their personalised floats while she waited, standing erect with an open towel in hand.

After a few minutes, the butler appeared again with two glasses of sugarcane juice.

"Tell your sahib to come quickly, or he will have to make a special appearance at the police station," Hasan said, gulping down the juice quickly.

Finally, Rambo arrived in his silk, Japanese-inspired house robe, his hair wet, and his hands wrapped in mittens. "Apologies, I was taking a shower."

They heard the soft shutting of a door and saw Avanti glide into the room effortlessly. She was in a pair of jeans and a simple white shirt.

"We are here to ask you some questions about the Chana murder case," Hasan said.

"Megh, the prime suspect in this case, claims that she was with you on a Farmers town hall when Chana died. She says that you asked her to accompany you."

Avanti slyly placed her hand and pressed Rambo's thigh, causing it to shiver uncontrollably. But in a surprise move, Rambo shoved it away.

"Yes, that is true. I am willing to attest in court if you like and all the farmers will gladly do the same," Rambo replied, looking Hasan straight in the eye.

"Well that settles it," Hasan was relieved.

"Another SGI death is terrible. It's that office, you see," Avanti said. "My father-in-law was initially looking at offices for CFC in that tower. But his Vaastu guide told him that the energies of that entire tower were completely messed up. Especially the two floors where the SGI have their offices. That's why he booked in Tower II; the Vaastu is so much better."

"Sujata, pay attention!" Avanti suddenly yelled as she spotted Vanilla trying to launch himself out of the float. "Did you take out their *nazar* today after they came back in?" she questioned Sujata, furrowing her high-arched eyebrows before turning back to the police officers.

"These things are not to be taken lightly. Even in numerology, SGI doesn't pass the test. How else do you explain two deaths?"

"Three actually," Rambo said quietly.

"Which one is the third?" Hasan asked.

"Not the third, the first one," Rambo corrected him.

"Which one?" Shreyas persisted.

"Toni Mehta, their son-in-law."

"But that happened some time ago," Hasan added.

"Yes, but the same company. He had his office there too."

"Lynching is not the same, Rambo. That was public anger," Avanti explained.

"Still a death, still murder," Rambo said, most profoundly. "Lynching is uncommon in the corporate world. There has been only one other such incident and that was in a Bengaluru-based company many years ago. It was a case of spurious milk powder that had killed many children. The mob had gone crazy."

"Bengaluru?" Hasan's ears perked up. "What was the name of the company?"

"It was not a chocolate company," Rambo continued.

"What was the name?"

"Magic Milk. It was a Dutch company. Sethji likes Dutch companies. Excellent investment. We had a lot of Magic Milk shares, but after that incident, the company's shares fell overnight. After that, SGI became the number one milk company as Magic Milk had to exit the Indian market. We lost a lot of money, close to…"

"Forget that!" Hasan said, growing restless. "Who got lynched?"

"I am sorry I don't know that," Rambo answered honestly.

"Don't be, you have told us a lot," Hasan said, jumping up from his sofa. "Shreyas, get up! We have to go now!"

A bewildered Shreyas gulped down the remainder of the juice and rushed behind Hasan.

"Sir, what happened?" Shreyas asked, panting, trying to keep up with Hasan as he raced towards the jeep in the driveway.

"Don't you see it?"

"What?"

"Doesn't it seem too much of a coincidence that in both cases, the victims of mob lynching incidents worked for consumer goods companies and that both incidents happened in Karnataka? And more importantly, Rambo said that after Magic Milk shut operations, SGI became number one. This, my boy, is a story of revenge," he said triumphantly.

Shreyas wanted Hasan to explain in detail, but he was already jabbing his phone.

"D'Souza?"

"Kya *yaar*! Already missing me?"

"There was a mob lynching incident in a company called Magic Milk in Bengaluru many years ago. I want you to find out the name of the person who got lynched."

"But why?"

"I have a feeling that my case here in Bombay is linked to this incident in Bengaluru."

"Your problem is that you have fallen in love with Bengaluru and are trying to find ways to connect everything back to it."

"D'Souza, get serious," Hasan said quietly.

"On it!" D'Souza sensed the seriousness in Hasan's voice.

"Can you also get me all details on Toni's lynching?"

"You will have it soon," he said, before hanging up.

Chapter 54
The Sardar Police Station

Mumbai, 20th July 2016

Shreyas entered the police station with smug content as he had made good progress on Chana's case. He was stoked about the breakthrough and wanted to share his intel with Hasan. But the colour almost drained from his face when he saw Hasan behind bars.

"Sir?" he said, the panic rising in his voice.

"Ah Shreyas, good that you are back. Locking myself up helps me concentrate," he pointed to a pile of dog-eared paperwork.

"But where are the goons?" Shreyas asked.

"Sir sent them to the new library they built as a part of the renovation! At least someone will utilise that space now," said a constable triumphantly.

"The lock-up is also keeping him safe," remarked another constable peering out a window.

"From who?" Shreyas inquired.

"*Morchas* are lining up outside our station. Look, there is one from IIIA."

"What's that?"

"The Italians in India Association," the constable said. "They are demanding the safety of Italians living here. I didn't even know Chana was Italian!"

"Part Italian, as we all are learning now. Anyway, what do you have on Chana?" Hasan asked, chewing the end of a pencil with concentrated fervour.

"One of my men has a lead," Shreyas stated proudly. "He has two witnesses who confirm that they saw a man enter Chana's building; they will give their descriptions to the sketch artist."

"Excellent! Get moving on that quickly."

"Sir, I also have some news," the ASI reported, walking towards the cell.

Shreyas sensed a renewed energy. He was discovering cops of all ranks at the station. Everyone was working way beyond their hours, even spending nights at the station. Hasan was relentless in his determination to succeed. It was as if he had a personal score to settle with himself.

"SGI has engaged The Urban Planters company. They maintain their indoor and outdoor plants for them," the ASI continued. "The morning of Surya's death, before the news broke out, their team had come to water the plants, and one of the gardeners took a potted plant with him as he needed to change the soil. That pot was right on the edge of the terrace from where Surya fell. He came today to return the pot, and SGI called us."

"Send the pot to Kaushal at the forensics lab. I don't know what prints he will find on it now after so many days," Hasan scoffed. "Tell him to have his best man on the job."

The night in the station passed quickly. Shreyas was sipping his sweet milk chai when the phone vibrated in his pocket. He knew it would be the Commissioner of Police calling for Hasan. Just moments before, he had seen the commissioner's number flash on Hasan's phone, which he had ignored. He implored Hasan to take the call. Shreyas could overhear snippets of their conversation. There was a certain deference in the commissioner's tone, as if he had just discovered Hasan's credibility. Suddenly Hasan's phone rang. It was D'Souza.

"Sir, I have to go," Hasan said abruptly, hanging up on the commissioner, and putting D'Souza on speaker instead.

"The person at Magic Milk who got lynched was a Dr Narain – the main food scientist. After this incident, the company had to wind up their operations. They had filed a police case saying that they were innocent and that they were being framed, but nothing happened. There was a story floating that SGI had adulterated Magic Milk's powder to kill their number one competition, but that story got squashed quickly."

"I think Megh is this Dr Narain's daughter. Her father did not die in an accident in California; he was killed here."

"How can you be so sure? Look, his last name is Narain, and her maiden name is Madan."

"She could have changed it."

"All of them changed their names? Priya is her aunt. Her name is also Madan, you think she also changed it?" Suddenly D'Souza yelled, "Wait wait! Megh Narain? When we were reading the names of students at St Joseph's School, there was a Megha Narain there!"

"Yes !" Hasan said, thumping the table with his fist.

"But PM said that Megh went to a school in Panchgani? "

"She could be lying. It is possible that Megha Narain is Megh Madan, and she studied here in St Joseph's in Bengaluru with Ali. Then she changed her name. She wanted revenge from the Jains for what SGI did to her father, and maybe even from Ali. Get me a picture of this Dr Narain! We have seen what Megh's father looked like in the picture at Priya Madan's house. We can confirm if it's the same person"

"I am on it!" D'souza screamed at one of his constables, "*Dei,* get me this man's picture!"

"Oh, and I almost forgot, I have just emailed you the telephone records from Toni's phone."

"Good, good. D'Souza, now you can also finally claim that you did some work in your career."

"Keep your phone close to you; I will call you once I have an update!" D'souza yelled before hanging up.

Hasan's phone rang again in the early hours of the morning.

"Saala!" D'Souza roared. "You were right! I just got the pictures from our files. It's the same fellow! Dr Narain is Megh's father."

Chapter 55
Families

Mumbai, 21st July 2016

"Megh, I know the truth about your father, about Dr Narain," Hasan said, looking at her, his gaze unwavering.

Shreyas could see Megh's shoulder muscles stiffen underneath her workout clothes. Her face suddenly looked tired.

"It's an admirable act of revenge, but three deaths will put you behind bars for many lifetimes," he said.

"I didn't kill anyone," she said quietly.

"And you really want me to believe you?"

"But that is the truth," she said, meeting his gaze. "I will admit that I was involved in the ADR scandal, but I didn't kill anyone."

"So ADR was your revenge?"

"It was meant to, but it clearly didn't work," she scorned.

"Why did you change your last name?"

"We had to, to save ourselves from getting killed."

"What do you mean?"

"When dad took us to India for our summer holidays, both Sid, my younger brother, and I were thrilled. It was the first time we were visiting India after mom's death. We were staying at my aunt's – you've already met PM – Priya maasi. Yes, she is my *maasi*, my mother's sister; not my father's. It was time for us to head back to LA, but one day, dad came back and surprised us.

"He told us that he had decided to relocate the family to India because he had found a job with a Dutch company called Magic Milk. I tried to protest, but it fell on deaf ears. Sid was excited to move to India, but I was not. I had my reasons. I had started suspecting that Dad and PM were in love. I was too young to realise that my mother and father had a failed marriage. I started detesting PM, but there was nothing I could do. Dad got us both enrolled in local schools. He took up the job at Magic Milk where he had an assistant, Jean. Jean's Nigerian husband had abandoned her. Ali, her son, was getting bullied in his public school because of the colour of his skin, so dad spoke to the principal of my school and got Ali transferred there. Jean was not sure how she would pay the fees, but Dad took care of it. Ali and I soon became good friends.

"Dad and Sid started to settle down, but I continued to hate PM more everyday, as she pretended to be a model housewife. When we first arrived in India, I used to sleep with her, while Sid would sleep in the other room with Dad. But one day, I saw her heading into his room while she thought I was asleep. The following day, I confronted Dad, and I was nasty to him and her. He slapped me.

"That day, I waited for school to get over. I wanted to apologise to him when I got home. But that was the day my father was lynched at the milk factory. Killed in public. Jean, his assistant, came to pick me from school. The police were everywhere. I didn't have a chance to make up to my father, to hug him.

"As the only surviving relative, PM legally adopted both of us. We received constant death threats as people were angry. It was understandable; many innocent children had died; they wanted revenge and still held Dad responsible for the batch of spurious milk powder. PM thought it would be best to conceal our identity. That's how we took her and my mother's last name – Madan – as our own.

"PM has done a lot for me. She had always loved my father, but had not expressed anything till after my mom passed away. It took me a long time to come around and see her as an independent person, separate from her relationships, but I eventually did.

"I was always a good student. I excelled in college. I also wanted to become a food scientist, like my father. Perhaps, this was my way of saying sorry to him. After a few years, we moved to Mumbai. Ali had moved here too. Over time, Ali and I reconnected through social media. Our childhood friendship rekindled, and he got friendly with Sid as well. Moving to Mumbai was overwhelming for me, but Ali had fitted in well. He was a popular face amongst Mumbai's elite. I thought Sid was doing fine. I was too caught up with my life to realise that he had fallen in bad company. He got into drugs. One day, Ali called me in the middle of the night. He told me to come immediately to a prominent Mumbai hotel. He was with a friend whom he introduced as Ashok Jain. He rushed me to a small backroom where I saw Sid sprawled on the floor. He was completely wasted. I took him home in a cab, but on the ride home, Sid kept blabbering something about this Ashok Jain.

"I could not make any sense of what he was saying. I tried to probe the next day, but he refused to divulge any information. PM and I sent Sid off to rehab. I was curious to know what was Sid's connection with Ashok. I pestered Ali, and he told me that Sid and Ashok had dated each other briefly before Sid started avoiding Ashok. That night in the hotel, a drunk Sid bumped into Ashok and got abusive. He started yelling at him. Ashok, a powerful man, threatened to get him arrested. That's when Ali had called me. I was shocked. I had no idea about any of this. My introverted, shy brother was having an affair with a man old enough to be his father? And that he had assaulted him? Every time I asked Sid about that incident, he would completely shut down.

"After a couple of months, we got a call from the rehab centre that Sid had committed suicide. He left me a letter explaining how Ashok had told him during a particularly vulnerable moment that his family had been involved in sabotaging a Dutch company that had been their biggest competitor. Ashok obviously didn't know who Sid was, but Sid learned the role Ashok Jain and SGI had played in our father's death. When Sid found out the truth, he couldn't forgive himself for being with Ashok, for pleasing him, for taking his gifts. His suicide note ended with : 'I feel dirty'."

"I was angry. The floodgates had opened, and all that I had suppressed for so many years came out as rage. The Jains had killed my dad, and now my brother was gone too. I wanted revenge, but I didn't know how. Slowly, a plan started to form in my head. The plan was to work for them and make their star product fail. Do to SGI what they had done to Magic Milk. Ali had not forgotten what my dad had done for him, and he was only too happy to help. The first step was to work for SGI, so I started keeping a tab of open vacancies in their company.

"The next step was to get closer to Surya Jain. He had just joined the family business and wanted to prove his worth. I knew Avanti through some of my friends, and I was aware that she and Surya hung around in the same social circles. I befriended her and got invited to one of her parties the night before my interview with SGI. I was hoping Surya would come and I could impress him so that he would remember me the following day when I interviewed with SGI. He came. It was the first time I met Surya, but that night I also met Aadi and lost my heart to him. But then I missed my interview because of the car accident."

She went quiet and clutched her hands around the arms of her chair as if bracing herself for what she was about to say next.

"So contrary to what you think, officer, I didn't have an affair with Surya. I hated him. On the day of D'sire's success party, when Surya said he was in love with me and hinted at a relationship, I truly understood what Sid had meant by dirty – I felt dirty too. Still, I decided to stay and put up with his advances, as I wanted our plan to succeed.

"Though I got the job based on my merit, Ali's resume was engineered to SGI's requirements. It was easy. We manufactured the best chocolate with no ADR in it, and that's the D'sire that became a hit. Yes officer, my D'sire was clean. That had been my idea. It was very rewarding to see my idea work. D'sire won all the awards, but we had to kill our own baby. That was the original plan after all, so we made one batch that was contaminated and sent that to the food authorities ourselves. That created havoc. Ali escaped to Lagos as planned and started blackmailing Ashok with their nude pictures and videos. We *wanted* an investigation as Ali would definitely be a suspect, and when they would search his desk, they would find that everything had been deleted. The CCTV footage would show Ashok deleting the evidence. Either Ashok would admit to conspiring in the ADR scandal to cover up for his sexual escapades, or if he spoke the truth, his illicit affairs would be enough to tarnish SGI's image. Both ways, SGI would suffer.

"For a while, everything was going as planned. I convinced Surya that Ali was responsible for the ADR scandal, we got the CCTV footage, and Surya saw with his own eyes that his father had deleted the evidence. He confronted Ashok and as expected, to hide his secret, he admitted to colluding with Ali, but somehow the internal investigation report showed Toni's name and he got lynched. Everything backfired, and nothing happened to the Jains."

"So you didn't get your revenge, *and* you murdered Surya?" Hasan intervened.

"Officer, have you ever wanted something badly, only to feel nothing when you finally got it?"

Hasan closed his eyes and replied, "Yes."

"I felt the same way. After that, I felt nothing except that I was tired. I was tired of living a lie. I wanted to go on with my life, and I didn't want anything to do with the Jains. So I moved on. I am not a murderer."

"Then what were you doing on the terrace of the SGI office when Surya died?" Shreyas asked quietly, looking Megh in the eye. She held his gaze.

"What do you mean?" she asked, stoically.

"I have just received a message from the forensic team that they found a footwear print on a pot on Surya's terrace. It is the print of ASICS. That's the brand that you wear, right?"

Megh's face turned red.

"So Megh, why did you go to Surya's office on the day of his death?" Hasan's voice echoed through her marble-floored living room.

"He called me.'"

"What?" Shreyas yelled in disbelief. He could not believe he had got Megh to confess.

"I had found out that evening about Aadi's affair, and I had gone for my run when Surya called me out of the blue. He was livid and dead drunk; he called me names. He said he had found out something about Ali and me. I reasoned with him to give me a chance to explain. He told me to come to his office right away.

"A lot of things were running through my mind. I had just learned of Aadi's affair; I now needed my career more than ever. I didn't know what exactly Surya had found out, but he could get me into trouble. I couldn't afford another blemish on my record, so I decided to go. When I got to the office building, I realised that the main entrance was closed as it was way past working hours. So I took the retail complex entrance to the office.

"I called Surya, and he came and swiped me in. He was very calm – punch drunk – but calm. He took me to the terrace and said that he had heard his grandfather yell at his father yet again. He broke into their closed-door meeting to intervene. MJ was upset as he had seen Ashok get *fresh* with another employee. Surya got upset with MJ for humiliating Ashok. It was the first time the grandfather and the grandson argued. MJ called him later and told him how he had to get Ali killed as he had learned about Ashok and Ali's affair. He also had Ali's call logs that showed that Ali had been in touch with me, even from Lagos. Surya thought I had slept with Ali. What angered him even more was that I had refused his advances.

"I told him everything about Magic Milk, my father, and my brother. I showed him my locket, which I always wear, containing the ashes of my family, but he felt nothing. I still remember what he said: '*Your father was an idealistic idiot, your brother a junkie, and you, you are a slut, Megh!*"

"That moment, I wanted to kill him, but I didn't. I realised that I had made a huge mistake by going to his office. I saw no point in talking to him, so I left."

"How?"

"I opened the terrace door, went down the stairs, opened the complex entrance and left."

"How come there are no fingerprints? Did you wipe them?" Hasan asked her.

"No, I wasn't thinking of fingerprints or footprints," she said, looking at Shreyas with contempt.

"It means that someone went in after you and wiped down the prints," Hasan said, thinking aloud.

"Which means he didn't fall off. Why were you hiding this?" Hasan asked her.

"Would anyone have believed me?"

"Hang on a second. So if Surya let you in with his key," Shreyas said slowly, "it is possible that he let the murderer in too."

"That means he knew the murderer," Hasan concluded sombrely.

"*Bhenchod!* What was that about the shoe print?" Hasan demanded as soon as the vault-like private elevator of Emporis ensconced them.

"I didn't receive any call from forensics. I took a chance," Shreyas said proudly.

"What a brilliant strategy," Hasan admitted, shaking his head in disbelief.

"It was the last ball, I had to try a sixer. The footprint on the pot was going around in my head. I knew if I could convince her that we had some forensic clue, she would tell the truth," he declared. "You think she is still hiding something?" he added worriedly.

"No," Hasan replied thoughtfully. "Now we need to find out who the other person was who went there after Megh. Whoever that was also killed Chana. What's happening with the sketch?" he demanded, suddenly a sense of urgency in his voice.

"My men are on it sir; they have a strong lead. Hopefully, we will nab the culprit soon."

Vilas pulled up with an unusual passenger in the front seat. It was a square-shaped box wrapped in gift-wrapping paper.

"What's that?" Hasan asked.

"Gift?" Vilas replied hesitantly.

"What gift?"

"For Shreyas' daughter? We are going for the naming ceremony, sir," he said.

"Sir, you forgot?" Shreyas exclaimed in disbelief, looking at Hasan's blank face. "I reminded you yesterday! I know the case is important, but Aai said today is the only auspicious day, or else the baby cannot have a name this year," he explained. "It's a very small affair, sir; only family. I would be honoured if you could come. *You* are her family."

They arrived in Mumbai's Girgaon precinct, where Shreyas lived with his family in the Khetwadi Chawl. Passing through a courtyard in the centre of six buildings, Hasan noticed an elaborate arrangement underway. The caterers and decorators were adding the final touches for a hundred guests plus party. A zealous emcee was repeatedly slapping the large booming speaker until it was ready to talk, and a group of ladies were rehearsing their steps to a famous Hindi song.

"There seems to be a big party in your neighbourhood. Won't that disturb your baby?" Hasan asked.

"This is *our* party, sir," Shreyas said cheerfully.

Escorted to the corner *kholi* by Shivu, the only such chamber in their building to have an inbuild bath and toilet, they walked through the living room, and passed the plywood partition wall to enter the sanctum of the baby. Hasan found Aai seated against a wall with her legs outstretched. Little Mithali, waiting to be officially named, was lying on her grandmother's legs close to her ankles and was being thoroughly massaged. Hasan looked around and found that the whims of infancy had claimed the room. The gears belonging to the unnamed small body occupied the entire place.

They moved to the courtyard where the celebrations were about to begin when Shreyas' phone rang.

"Sir, they got them, the person who killed Chana," he said to Hasan.

Chapter 56
The Culprit

Mumbai, 22nd July 2016

Shreyas trailed behind Hasan as he jumped off from the moving jeep. The security guard guided them to the outhouse.

"Bhenchod! Where is everyone?" Hasan hollered at the guard.

"There is a big puja going on for Surya bhaiya's *shanti*. They told me to tell you to wait in the outhouse; they will come soon, sir."

Shoving the startled guard, Hasan strode towards the living room, where the chanting stopped immediately as the police made an appearance.

"We're here to arres—"

"What nonsense is this, Officer?" Ashok shouted. He sprung up and marched towards them.

"Officer, please come with me to the outhouse," a voice from behind startled them.

They turned to see a frail MJ seated in a wheelchair. "I will come with you," he added. Bhanu, seated beside him, also sprung up and got ready to roll his wheelchair forward.

Shreyas was taken aback by their reaction. Even when the truth had finally found its way and had come knocking on Zanara's doorsteps, the inhabitants were more interested in keeping it at an arm's distance, in the outhouse.

"No, this, here, is good," Hasan said, waving at the attendees, "actually this is perfect," he continued as he spotted the Samsungs and the iPhones hoisted in the air to record the proceedings.

"First, let's start with the murder of Toni Mehta."

"Murder of Toni Mehta?" repeated Kabir from the front row.

"Yes, your father was murdered by none other than your grandfather MJ."

Hasan could hear everyone gasping.

"Just around the time of the D'sire scandal, MJ learned that Toni was siphoning funds from the company. MJ had been tolerating Toni's illicit affairs, but this was too much for him. When the scandal happened, MJ manipulated the internal report and paid off some goons to murder Toni at the milk factory and make it look like lynching. This incident let him get rid of Toni forever; it also let him hide Ashok's affair with Ali. Of course, organising lynching attacks was nothing new for MJ. After all, he had done it many years ago when he killed Dr Narain at Magic Milk. That is how SGI became the number one milk company, by conspiring against Magic Milk and forcing them to exit India in their early years. Megh joined SGI to avenge her father, Dr Narain's death and her brother, Sid's, suicide," he said, looking at Ashok.

"You knew about Ali?" Ashok asked MJ, who continued to look down at his hands.

"Yes Ashok, he did," Hasan continued. "What he did not know was that Toni had suspected MJ and had shared his doubts with his wife," he added slowly.

A strange silence enveloped the room. All eyes fell upon Bhanu as she lovingly fixed MJ's hair. Wrapping her pallu tightly around her body, she began wistfully, "All along, my entire life, I have done what my Babuji wanted. First, he forced me to marry Toni. Then when things were not working out between us, he forced me to pretend that everything was normal. And after Toni's death, he insisted that I moved back in here to take care of all of them, including this villager Sharda, who behaves as if I am the maid.

"Toni had called me the morning before he died. He became suspicious when he learned that there was a report stating he had sanctioned the use of ADR. There was fear in his voice, and this time, I believed him. He was a staunch vegetarian. He could be a womaniser, but he could never do something like this. He knew someone in the company was setting him up. He told me he suspected that it was MJ. At first, I didn't believe him. I didn't want to believe that my Babuji could do this," she paused.

"Toni was a loving father, and we both had big dreams for our Kabir. That's why I kept quiet even after Toni's death. I wanted Kabir to get his due share in SGI. Babuji had promised me that if SGI bagged the new telecom venture, it would be his graduation gift to Kabir. I was so happy. Surya would be taking my father's place, and my Kabir would be the head of the telecom business. But at the tula daan ceremony, he cheated Kabir and announced Surya as the head of the telecom business instead. All my life, I have had to play second fiddle. I couldn't let that happen to my Kabir. He was smarter, better, and more deserving than that drug addict Surya.

"I was so mad after the puja. I called Surya and told him I wanted to meet him; it was urgent. He was very nice to me. He told me to come to his office. I wore Nasima's burqa and left the house as Nasima. Nasima has a problem – she gets night terrors sometimes, so she sleeps with me. Nobody knows; it's our little secret. She doesn't remember anything the morning after the episode. The tula daan evening, I slipped her a few sleeping pills without her knowledge and in the morning, I told her that she had gone to the market as usual, and had experienced an episode in the night. I even showed her the grocery bill. She believed me and didn't ask any questions.

"Dressed in a burqa as Nasima, I went with the driver to the market as usual. He kept chatting, but I told him I didn't feel too well and didn't talk much throughout the ride. I got down at the market entrance, quickly took a cab, and went to the office from the retail entrance. Surya let me in. He seemed drunk, but somehow in control of his senses. I told him I needed some fresh air, and we went to the terrace. I told him about Toni, and about Babuji killing him. I went to the edge of the terrace pretending to jump off the ledge and kill myself. He ran after me and in the shuffle, I pushed him off. I smashed his phone, wiped away the fingerprints, and left. Then I took a cab back to the market, picked up the order that I had placed over the phone, and left in the car for home."

"I can't believe you would do that!" MJ's voice trembled. "Kill your own nephew! Kill my grandson! You and your son do not deserve a single penny. I intend to leave *everything* to Ashok!"

"You know Ashok's capabilities," she smirked at him. "'You have no faith in him, why else would you hand the business to Surya? The business will be in Kabir's hands. The news of Ashok's affairs and what you and he did to Magic Milk will be all over the media tomorrow. They're doing that for me," she said, pointing towards the phones recording her.

"And you Babuji, you are old and frail. How long will you even live? I am still giving you those potassium tablets, despite your levels being high. That was the reason I had to get rid of your silly PA Chana as well."

MJ was stunned. Sharda, Ashok and Kabir looked on, as if in a trance.

"She was going to show Babuji's medication, including the potassium tablets, to the company doctor. He would have figured out that something was wrong. When I visited the office, I saw she was upset over some email she had received from Megh. I figured if I got her out of the way, the blame would very conveniently fall on Megh."

"So you approached the liftman of Imperial Towers I to help you out?" Hasan asked in admiration.

"No," she laughed, "he approached me."

"He told me that he had seen Ashok and one employee make out. He wanted me to give him some baksheesh for sharing information. I also learned that he was taking money from both, Ashok and that employee to keep his mouth shut. He didn't seem like he would have an issue doing a job for me for some quick cash. I have no remorse and am happy to go to jail, but Kabir is innocent. He will not play second fiddle to anyone and will remain the sole heir of this business."

Chapter 57
Divine Retribution

"Officer, I am so happy to see that you could make it today," Megh said warmly.

"You look well," Hasan replied as she walked towards him. He hadn't met her in seven months since the SGI case had wrapped up. Wearing a sharp business suit with a perky red lipstick, she exuded confidence. Hasan was taken aback by her gesture of familiarity as she bent forward and planted a kiss on his cheek, freeing the heart-shaped locket from the smocking of her bodice that began to dance between them.

"I see you still wear your locket," he commented.

"Yes, I had misplaced it, but I am glad I found it," she said. "It somehow anchors me."

Hasan understood exactly what she meant. In one lifetime, Megh had lived many lives assuming different identities in different stories, but there was one story that was so powerful that it overshadowed everything else and shaped most of her life's decisions. Megh had stuffed that story in that locket.

"It's quite a lavish party here," Hasan commented.

"It's our CEO's first public event," she said, pointing to a corporate banner with Rambo's face plastered on it. "Come on! Let's get you a drink."

Hasan recognised a few faces on his way to the bar. Sethji was engaged in a conversation with the Maharani of Jamshedpur's stunning necklace, and Avanti was enthralling her all-male audience, who were buzzing around her like moths.

"So tell me about this event? What's it about?"

"I won't reveal many details, just that CFC is unveiling its most ambitious chocolate. We have tried to make a chocolate with a conscience. It is not going to eradicate all the evil that plagues the chocolate industry, but we are doing our bit."

"What do you mean?"

"Not many know that the chocolate that they eat is mostly tainted. Chocolate is made from the cacao bean (cocoa) that grows primarily in the tropical climates of West Africa and Latin America. West Africa collectively supplies two-thirds of the world's cocoa crop. The cocoa they grow and harvest are sold to a variety of chocolate companies, including some of the world's largest. But the children who work on these farms live in deplorable conditions. Some children end up at these cocoa farms because they need work, and they are told the pay is good. Other children are sold by their own relatives to traffickers or to the farm owners. Once on the cocoa farms, the children may not see their families for years."

"This happens even today?"

She nodded. "Representatives of some of the biggest and best-known brands of international chocolates cannot guarantee that their chocolate is child labour free. Virtually every child has scars on the hands, arms, legs, or shoulders from accidents with the machete used to strike the cocoa pods.

"In addition to that, children are also commonly exposed to very dangerous pesticides that are sprayed copiously on cocoa farms. These children live in absolute destitute circumstances for months and years. Most of these children working on cocoa farms have never eaten chocolate in their lives."

"Wow, human greed has no limit," Hasan said.

"Not everyone or every company is like that; some companies are doing good work too," she said. "What we are trying to do is spread awareness. I think we better move inside as the event is about to kick off."

Hasan found himself a seat at the end of the hall. From the corner of his eye, he saw Megh stand against a wall with her phone camera focused on Rambo as he took centre stage. She beamed with the pride of a parent who was about to see her child perform on stage for the first time.

"Good evening, ladies and gentleman," Rambo's voice boomed throughout the room. "Thank you for turning up in such large numbers. I have a question for all of you. Are you willing to pay a little more for your chocolate?"

Hasan did not know this Rambo. He squinted his eyes to get a closer look at him. Rambo had lost more hair, and gained a bit of weight around his belly, but there was something else about him. He realised that no gloves were engulfing his hands. This Rambo was different; he was willing to bear his flaws and reveal himself.

"Today, CFC is announcing the launch of the first fair-trade compliant and slave-free chocolate in India. It's called Divine. Manufactured in India, this chocolate is produced without exploiting the farmers. It is India's first mass-produced ethical chocolate.

"However, the success of the programme will depend greatly on the genuine support of the consumers. Only when the consumers are educated and insist on fair-trade and slave-free chocolate will the right kind of chocolate be manufactured and find its way in people's houses," Rambo continued passionately.

"Because the extra money that you will pay won't probably affect you, but it will do a lot for the farmers and their families."

"He's impressive, isn't he?" Megh whispered to Hasan as the event came to a close.

Hasan nodded, "Yes, I didn't think he would support such an initiative."

"Good men sometimes come in strange packages," Megh commented. "Officer, that goes for you too."

The last of the guests left, and the event was officially a wrap. Waiting for her Uber ride at the porch, Megh spotted a proud Sethji pat Rambo on his back. Her hands immediately reached for her locket. She understood the impact that pat had on his self-esteem.

In the car, her phone pinged. It was a message from Aadi. He wanted to know about the event.

Rambo was fantastic; he did a great job, she texted.

Don't forget to give yourself credit. You deserve it, he typed back.

She could see that Aadi was trying hard to salvage their relationship. Megh still loved him, but she didn't know if she wanted to be with him. There was so much that they didn't know and understand about each other.

The car stopped at a traffic light, and Megh saw the Imperial Towers shimmering in the moonlight. She stuck her head out of the window, and instinctively her gaze sought out the last floor of Imperial Towers I, the floor with the terrace, the floor with Surya's office.

"Madam, you know there was a gruesome murder that happened in this building a few months ago," the Uber driver said, startling Megh.

"Yeah, I remember reading something about it," she replied, sounding vague.

"Deadly it was, madam," he continued, enjoying his authority on the subject. "An aunt flung her nephew from that terrace and almost got away with it!" he said, pointing the building out to her.

"I remember reading that the police did a great job," Megh added. "You can hardly say she got away."

"I don't know what the truth is, but when I saw her picture in the papers, I could hardly believe it. So skinny and total *sati savitri* image as well. How could someone like her do something like that?"

The signal turned green, and the traffic light-induced conversation thankfully came to a stop. Megh's mind revisited the day Surya died.

She could hear his words so clearly as if he was sitting next to her in the car.

Your father was an idealistic idiot, your brother a junkie and you – you are a slut, Megh.

She could still taste the bile that had come up her mouth. She remembered leaving his office and taking the fire exit stairs when she realised that her locket was missing. It probably fell off when she was showing it to Surya. She vaulted up the stairs all the way back to the fiftieth floor and called him. His phone was dead. She knocked on his door and waited for a while when she noticed that it was not shut correctly. She pushed it open and headed to the terrace, and that's when she heard him. He was dangling from the ledge and screaming for help. But no one could hear him or help him. She picked up her locket from the ground and pushed him down the ledge. She wiped the fingerprints on her way out.